CINNAMON BUN BESTIES

Curl up with all of the SWIRL novels!

Pumpkin Spice Secrets by Hillary Homzie
Peppermint Cocoa Crushes by Laney Nielson
Cinnamon Bun Besties by Stacia Deutsch
Salted Caramel Dreams by Jackie Nastri Bardenwerper

CINNAMON BUN BESTIES

Stacia Deutsch

Sky Pony Press
New York

Chapter One
CARD CLASH

Monday, January 31
Two weeks until Valentine's Day

"I'll do it, Mrs. Choi." I raised my hand. To make certain that my teacher saw me, I waved. My heavy bracelet jingled like tiny bells as the charms smacked against each other. I loved that sound. It energized me to shake my hand a little harder. "I want to be in charge of this year's Cupid Candy Cards."

I knew the job was already mine, but Mrs. Choi took her time looking around at the other students on the Fort Lupton Middle School student council. We were a small group of representatives from the sixth, seventh, and eighth grades. Two boys and two girls were voted in from each grade, and this was the second time I'd been voted by my classmates to be on the council. Last year in sixth grade, when I worked on the Valentine's Day Cupid Candy Cards fund-raiser, we made the most money for the school in the history of the project. No joke. That was awesome.

And because we made so much money, the middle school spring dance was epic. We paid for an amazing DJ! She played the best music, threw out lighted necklaces, and gave everyone these funny socks to slip around in.

No one said it out loud, but I knew that because of all my hard work, I'd get to lead the Cupid Cards project this time around.

"Thanks for stepping up, Suki," Mrs. Choi said when no one else volunteered to be the coordinator. She had a pencil tucked over her ear. Pushing back her short brown hair, she tugged it out and made a note on a pad of paper. "Is there anyone else who—"

With a *whoosh* and a *bang*, the door to the classroom swung open. "Sorry I'm late." Joshua Juaquin hurried into the room and settled himself into an empty seat at the back. JJ was one of the boys voted in from my class. "I was playing soccer and lost track of time." Student council met at the end of lunch. Typical JJ, trying to squeeze too many activities into his lunch break.

When I glanced over my shoulder at him, I could see JJ's cheeks were flushed pink and there were beads of sweat in his short brown hair. JJ caught me staring, so he winked. I rolled my eyes at him and quickly turned away.

"No problem. We were just getting started. Welcome, JJ." Even the teachers called him that. I think it took the pressure off everyone, since his mom was the mayor. If no one said his last name out loud, they could forget about the connection.

"Now, where were we?" Mrs. Choi looked down at a piece of paper on her desk. "Oh, right, Suki Randolph wants to lead the Cupid Card Commit—" Our teacher hadn't even finished the sentence when JJ's hand shot up.

With a deep breath, I twirled a strand of my long, straight, black hair and closed my eyes. I knew exactly what was about to happen. This wasn't the first time that JJ had challenged me for something important. It was, in fact, the eighth time. Not that I'm keeping score, or anything petty like that. And to be perfectly honest, some of those times, I'd challenged *him*.

"I want to lead the Cupid Notes project," JJ proclaimed.

"It's 'Cupid *Cards*,'" I hissed under my breath. Then, louder, I exclaimed, "Ouch," when I got kicked in the leg.

"Shhh, Suki," Marley Renault whispered.

My next-door neighbor and best friend, Marley, was sitting next to me. She was also on the council. I was tall and a little out of shape with slightly tan skin and very straight hair, whereas Marley was super skinny, short, with very dark skin, and had this insane mess of hair that stood out at all angles. Years ago, we bonded over the fact that neither of us could do anything nice with our hair. Complaining brought us together.

"Suki," Marley whispered, leaning in toward me. "JJ is going after *your* job."

"I know," I whispered back. "I hate him."

I said that a lot, and Marley always replied, "There's not much space between love and hate." That's a line from some song Marley likes. Marley said it fit for me and JJ. She insists I've had a crush on him since fourth grade.

She's wrong. Even though I love Valentine's Day, I'm not interested in romance. I like the idea of falling in love and all that stuff, but when I'm older, for sure not now. I have better things to do, and a boyfriend would take up too much time. I'd seen what could happen. A long time ago, there were four of us who were besties, two of them started "dating" and totally betrayed us. Even though we were still in the same school, we hadn't all been friends again ever since.

Besides, who would I want to date? Certainly not JJ.

"No love," I assured her. "My heart is a bottomless black hole for JJ."

"Yeah, right. Whatever." Marley leaned back in her chair, her head bobbing softly to whatever musical tune was rolling through her brain. Probably one she was making up. She made up a lot of songs.

"We all know why Suki wants the coordinator position," Mrs. Choi told JJ. "But why do you want it, JJ?" She pinned him with a serious stare and said, "Convince me."

Instead of him looking at our teacher, I swore I could feel beams from JJ's eyes shooting darts at the back of my head. My skin prickled.

"Valentine's Day is my favorite holiday," JJ began.

I wanted to leap up out of my chair and shout "Liar!" But that wouldn't be cool. Besides, I didn't actually know what his favorite holiday was, since I'd barely talked to him in the past three years. Still, the chance that it was Valentine's Day was really small.

I tapped my fingers on the desk in front of me while he went on.

"Honestly, I've never led anything like this before, but I think I could do a good job. I have a few ideas on how to raise more money."

"Impossible," I muttered.

The cards worked like this: It cost students a dollar to send a heart-shaped card with a lollipop to anyone at school. That was a Cupid Card. Buyers could send them to a friend, a crush, a teacher . . . anyone. All student council members got excused from fourth period class so the cards could all get delivered. And the cards—paper heart and attached candy—only cost ten cents each to make, so we turned a 90 percent profit! Last year we raised over $300 to use for the school's spring dance. That was enough for the DJ, but there was no way we could ever top last year. I was only hoping to match our sales.

"We can double our take," JJ told the council. "The dance this year will be extra-epic! We can have a live band instead of a boring DJ, professional dancers to teach us moves, and get some kickin' prizes for the best moves." He wiggled in his seat, slamming his head toward the desk, as if that was some kind of dancing.

"Wrong," I blurted out. I reined my tone in to a calm voice and told JJ, "You're wrong."

Mrs. Choi stopped me. "Suki, obey the rules of respect, please. You can share your opinion, but do it nicely." Mrs. Choi was all about "self-empowerment and personal growth." There was a poster that said that on her classroom wall.

"Okay." I turned to JJ and said with a small smirk, "I respectfully disagree."

Though I was calm on the outside, my heart was beating hard against my ribs as I stood up to continue. I became very aware of my outfit—black leggings with holes in the knees and an *I ♥ dogs* sweatshirt that my mom bought for me. The shirt was a little cheesy, but it's true. I do heart dogs.

My skin felt hot and scratchy under that sweatshirt as I stared at JJ.

"Your idea won't work," I protested, and began to make my case like a TV lawyer. "Last year we sold three hundred and fifty cards." Since I'd worked on the project and JJ hadn't, I added, "We maxed out. Kids won't buy more than that. It's not like every kid in the school buys them. Some can't afford them. Some don't want to give them out. Some think Valentine's Day is dumb. Some—"

It was as if I hadn't spoken at all. "We could easily sell a thousand Candy Canes this year," JJ argued, also standing up.

Augh! "Cards," I hissed this time out loud. "You don't even know what they are called! They're Cupid Cards!"

"A thousand Cupid Cards, then," he amended. "Think of all the money we'd make."

We both started doing the math at the same time. At a dollar a note, minus our cost . . .

"That means we'd earn . . ." I started.

"Nine hundred dollars," JJ finished. "Easy." *Ack.* How'd he get that math done before me? I knew I had a higher grade in math class than him. After our last quiz, I'd looked over our teacher's shoulder and peeked at her computer screen.

"There are only six hundred and fifteen kids in the school." I was gearing up to repeat myself, since he obviously hadn't heard me before. "Not everyone buys a card. Sure, some buy a few, but it's not nearly what you think."

"*I* can fix that," JJ insisted. His gaze was pinned on me, and it felt like the rest of the student council and our teacher weren't there anymore. There was a fire in his dull, bland eyes. "I bet we can sell way more than a thousand."

My voice rose as I argued against him. "You weren't involved last year, so you don't have a clue how this works." He hadn't been on student council, but now he was, in addition to being captain of the soccer team and a lead in the school play.

Some people thought it was because his mom was the mayor that JJ got pretty much anything he wanted. I didn't know what I thought about the impact of his mom. I mean, I would never say this out loud, but JJ was pretty good at everything he tried, so maybe he deserved it all.

At this moment, though, it didn't matter if his mom was Queen of the Entire Universe. He wasn't going to win this battle.

"We can—" he started.

"No way," I interrupted as I moved away from my desk and took a huge step toward him. "We'll never sell a thousand Cupid Cards!"

I flashed back to the end of the fifth-grade spelling bee when it was just me and him for the finals. I was sure I'd won it all when he got an easy word and stole the trophy. I got him back in the sixth-grade geography bowl. The smallest country on earth? He blew it. The answer was the Vatican. The trophy was mine!

For two people who barely spoke, we were incredibly competitive with each other.

He came toward me. "You're being a bummer, Suki."

That was a personal insult. Mrs. Choi probably should have jumped in, but she didn't. I'm sure she wanted us to "work it out," and was just watching to see what would happen. That was so like her!

"I'm not a *bummer*," I countered. "I'm realistic. You're such a dreamer, you think millions of Cupid Cards are going to magically appear at school and money for the dance will rain from the sky!"

"You—" he started.

"You—" I said at the same time.

"Enough!" Mrs. Choi ended the argument. I guess she'd decided we couldn't handle things after all.

I stepped back toward my desk and, with a final huff, turned away from JJ. My heart was beating hard. Arguing with raised voices wasn't my style. But, deep inside, I had to admit, it felt good to tell JJ what I was thinking. I wished I'd done that back in fourth grade, when this battle between us first started.

Mrs. Choi let a long silent pause hang in the air before peering at us both with those serious teacher eyes.

"Suki Randolph and Joshua Juaquin, you will work together to organize the Valentine's Day Cupid Candy Cards project. You don't have a lot of time, so get started right away." With a click of her tongue and a tough squint at each of us, Mrs. Choi made it clear that there was no further discussion on the point. Her decision was final. Right before she moved to the next item on the student council meeting agenda, she added, "Good luck."

Chapter Two
DOGGONE IT

Two dreadful hours later

"I hate him."

"Really? Are you sure about that?"

"*Ugh.*" I let out a huge sigh. My breath looked like smoke in the cool winter air. "Yes. Positive." I zipped up my coat.

Marley and I were walking home from school. I'd insisted we go through the park because I needed the extra time to blow off some steam. Plus, it was pretty where we lived—in a small city at the base of a mountain. The park was in the middle of our neighborhood.

There were apartments lining one side and houses on the other sides. Beyond those, streets with bigger houses fanned out in every direction.

In the center of the grassy area were benches and some very tall trees. At the far end was a really nice jungle gym and a fenced-in dog park. Even when I was little, I liked going there to watch the dogs running around and playing.

I've never had a dog, but it was still one of my favorite places in town.

Thinking that watching dogs play would shake my mood, I walked with Marley up to the wire fence and peered in. We didn't have snowy winters, but the afternoons could get really chilly this time of year. Today was pretty cold, so there was just one big dog running around.

A husky mix, I thought. I considered asking the owner—who was on a bench, looking at his phone—if I could toss the dog a stick. Playing with a dog seemed like a good idea. My whole body felt like it was tied in a giant knot. Mom was a yoga teacher, and I knew what she'd say about it, but I was sure that some deep breathing would *not* help this situation.

As I reached for the gate to the dog park, the owner called "Skylar! Come!" and the husky bounded over. They were leaving. Sigh. I was too late.

I stomped the ground as we left.

Turning to Marley, I asked, "Did you see the way JJ looked at me after Mrs. Choi said we'd have to work together?" I imitated his stupid grin. "I hate him."

Marley didn't respond, but I knew what her silence meant.

No. No. No! I didn't like JJ, no matter what she thought. Not even a tiny bit. I gagged loudly at the idea.

We walked in silence over the thick green grass, past the swing set, and onto the sidewalk on the other side.

"Can we go around again?" I asked Marley. I had homework waiting for me, but once across the park wasn't enough to calm me down. I was so mad, it would take a million miles of walking for me to feel normal.

"You're killing the grass with all that clomping," she responded, quickly singing out, "Like a single glove, the earth is crying for a little love . . ."

"Who wrote that?"

She rolled her eyes at me. "Me, of course."

"Not half bad." I shrugged, not sure I understood the connection between a glove and the earth, but Marley knew what it meant and that's all that mattered. It was her song. "Play it for me later?" I asked. That would get my mind off what happened at student council.

Marley couldn't resist sharing her music. She nodded and said, "We can video chat." Then she glanced at the time on her phone and said, "We should head home. There's homework to do and I have drum lessons tonight." She shoved her phone in her pocket and did an air drum thing with her hands, as if she was playing a big solo.

Even though her parents hoped Marley would be interested in medicine, like both of them, she dreamed about being in a rock band and was totally focused on that goal. She didn't just play drums—Marley sang in the school choir and was learning how to work a light and sound board that she'd bought on the Internet. And she was trying to start a neighborhood band that would practice in her garage on weekends and "play gigs" when they were ready. So far, the Happy Little Llamas was only two people, but they were looking for someone who played guitar to join. Soon, they'd be a real band.

I stood straighter as I said, "I bet JJ's not going to want to help organize the Cupid Cards once he finds out how much work it is. He'll probably quit."

"And leave you as the only leader?" Marley fake choked. "Don't count on it."

"*Bah.*" I stuck out my tongue. "Look who's being a 'bummer' now." I glanced at my best friend and frowned. "What am I going to do? I can't work with him!"

"You're gonna have to—" Marley stopped mid-thought as we reached our street. We lived on a cul-de-sac a few blocks from the park. I lived at the center of one end and her house was to the right of mine.

"Is that a dog barking?" I tipped my head and listened hard.

No one around us had a dog. Believe me, I would know. I'd been begging my parents to get me one for almost a year. They said I wasn't responsible enough. Mom wasn't home all day because she was teaching people how to bend into pretzel shapes, and Dad traveled for work as an engineer. Every time I asked, which was practically every day, the answer was

"No." All the promises in the world wouldn't change their minds.

"Hey, Marley, look!"

Suddenly the cutest little black puppy came running toward us. It was coming down the road fast, like a fuzzy bowling ball. I blinked as the puppy disappeared behind a tree.

"Stop, Luna! Stop! Come back! Whoa!"

I knew that voice.

My eyes went from the dog to my next-door neighbor. "Olivia," I said in greeting, raising my head in a slight nod. "Hey."

"Please stop her!" Olivia shrieked to me and Marley. "Help!" Then to the dog, "Luna, come back!"

Luna stopped to pee on Marley's lawn.

Marley and I looked at each other. We weren't friends with Olivia Dalton, but we couldn't let her dog run away. That would be mean.

"Here, Little Lu-Lu," Marley called. The dog ignored her. I bet she didn't know her name yet. And even if she did, Lu-Lu wasn't her name.

"Let's block her in," I suggested. "Chasing a dog just makes them run more."

We moved quickly, surrounding Luna as best as

we could, but she bolted away before we could grab her.

"Come back!" Olivia cried. Then she shrieked, "Car!" as a minivan turned onto the street. The car was nowhere near Luna, but we didn't want to take a chance with the next driver that came home.

"We've gotta get her fast," Marley said, watching the van disappear into a garage. She told Olivia, "I'll go left, you go right. Suki, you've got the middle."

"No." I had a different idea. "Be right back," I called out.

While Marley and Olivia chased Luna, I ran toward my house.

"Where are you going?" Marley called after me.

"Don't leave!" Olivia shrieked.

There wasn't time to explain. I ignored them both and kept going. Inside, I grabbed a long piece of string, a jar of peanut butter, and a spoon.

I was only gone a minute before I ran back outside.

"How could you ditch us?" Marley asked, glancing from Olivia to me and then to the dog, who was now a black dot at the far end of the street.

"I didn't ditch you," I replied. Music was Marley's thing. Dogs were mine. "I'd never leave Luna like that."

I tossed the string to Olivia. It was a little thicker than yarn. Olivia probably had a leash at home, but we were going to need something right away. When we caught Luna, she could tie an end to her collar to keep her close.

I sat down on my own porch step and opened the peanut butter jar. I scooped a spoonful.

"Come, Luna," I called out in my loudest and most authoritative voice.

I held out the spoon and waved it in the air so the peanut butter scent wafted toward the puppy.

She completely ignored me.

I had to admit to myself that this wasn't working the way I'd seen it on the Internet. Catching her might be harder than I thought . . .

Luna was still pretty far away, so I rose and slowly moved in, getting as close as Luna would let me. My bracelet charms jingled as I waved the spoon around some more.

"Come, Luna," I said again in a strong voice.

Luna dropped a stick from her mouth and sniffed the air. Now I had her attention, but what should I do next? I wanted to take a break, run back inside and watch the video I'd seen online again. The guy,

"Doug, the Dog-Talker," made it look so easy, and since I didn't have much experience with real dogs, his advice was all I had to go on. I was going to have to try harder with Luna.

With my hands on my hips, I demanded, "Come!" My tone made it clear that it wasn't a choice. It was a command.

She looked at me and took a few steps in my direction.

Excitement bubbled inside me, but I didn't let it show. I didn't want Olivia, or Luna, to think I was uncertain about what I was doing. "Come!" I said again firmly.

Luna moved slowly toward me, raising her head and, again, sniffing the air.

"If you want the snack, then you gotta come." As far as training goes, that was probably too many words, but now I felt like she was listening. I told her, "I'm taking you home." My feet began moving backward toward Olivia's house. Marley and Olivia were watching as I confidently rotated on my tennis shoe heel, turned my back to Luna, and walked down the street with the peanut butter–covered spoon hanging down by my side. With a quick look over my shoulder, I saw

Luna pause for a second, but then decide to follow me, nose raised, sniffing after the peanut butter.

When we reached Olivia's house, I sat down on the grass. Happiness washed over me as I finally let Luna lick the peanut butter. "Good puppy," I cooed while Olivia attached the string to Luna's collar.

"Thanks for getting her back," she told me. And to Marley, "Uh, thanks for trying."

"No problemo." Marley smiled, flashing her braces. Her rubber bands were red and yellow, same as her drum set.

"How'd you know about peanut butter?" Olivia asked me.

"Lucky guess." I shrugged.

Marley was the only one who knew about the research I'd been doing. It was our secret. It was part of my plan to prove to my parents, when the time was right, that I could handle having a dog. Today proved that I was ready! With Luna relaxing by my feet, I felt like a dog-training rock star.

"Hey, girls!" Marley's mom stuck her head out of the house. She was a barely bigger version of Marley. "Mar, time to go!"

"Yay!" Marley said, standing up, rolling some

invisible drum solo off her wrists. "Marley out." She
waved at Luna and said, "Adios, Suki. See ya, puppy."
She belted out a new rhyme, "Puppies run for fun . . .
and for fun, I run," as she dashed away.

Once Marley was gone, it was just me and Olivia. I
handed her the spoon, even though most of the peanut butter was gone. I didn't have anything to say, and
we both stayed quiet.

Olivia was one of the people who'd been a bestie,
but wasn't anymore. I was about to make up an excuse
and leave when I heard a voice shout:

"Oli-vi-a!"

I looked out to see JJ heading our way. I groaned.
He was the other piece of our old bestie group. He and
Olivia were still friends. Me and Marley were still
friends. The two groups never mixed. And as far as
I was concerned, no matter what Mrs. Choi wanted,
we'd never work together. Ever. Never. Never.

I gave JJ a long, bitter stare. He'd changed into
a collared shirt and khakis with a belt, and he was
wearing the new tennis shoes he'd bought last week.
(Not that I'm paying attention. I only knew they were
new because I'd heard him talking in the hall.) He
looked like he was going to play golf.

"'Sup, Suki?" he said, seeing me there.

I quickly stood. "Bye."

"You can stay if you want," Olivia said. I couldn't stand it when she was so friendly, which was pretty much always. It was like the past didn't matter to Olivia and she just went on, la-di-da, like nothing had happened.

JJ wasn't like that. He wasn't mean, but if he could beat me at something, anything, he took advantage of it. Mrs. Choi had thrown us together, but he was up to something. I could feel it. I just hadn't figured out his game yet.

"JJ and I are going to take Luna for a walk." Olivia handed me the string, with the dog attached at the end. "Here. Hold her. I'll get the leash."

Before I could protest, I was watching Luna while Olivia dashed into her house.

JJ and I were standing on the lawn. Just us.

I glared at him. He glared at me. Neither of us spoke.

It felt like a hundred years, though it was probably really about a hundred seconds, before Olivia came back. "Let's all walk around together," she said cheerily. Bending low, she replaced my string on Luna's collar with Luna's purple-glitter leash.

Did she really think we could go back in time? I shook my head. "No, thanks."

"Yeah, Suki's probably busy," JJ said. His straight teeth never needed braces. I was getting mine put on over the summer. I double-checked when he smiled. Yep. For sure, he'd never need them. It was another reason I hated him. "Let me know when you want to talk about the Candy Canes. I can tell you my ideas," he said coolly, and, again, I wondered what he was up to. How was he planning to show off and make me look bad? It was so frustrating that I couldn't figure it out!

"They're called Cupid Candy Cards," I said firmly. "C-A-R-D-S." I spelled it out. "Bye, Luna." I purposely didn't say anything else to JJ. Though I muttered, "Just quit already," loud enough for him to hear me.

I hurried across the lawn and dashed inside my house, slamming the door with a bang.

Chapter Three
PUPPY LOVE

Tuesday, February 1

The next day, I managed to avoid JJ all day at school. Until I knew what he was up to, I had to protect myself.

Marley saw me ducking around and called me a "baby," but I didn't care. I wasn't ready to face the inevitable. Working with him was going to be a disaster.

After the final bell, I met Marley at the coffee shop across the street from school. On Tuesdays, both our parents worked late, so we liked to hang out there and do homework.

We each ordered a Cinnamon Bun Swirl. It was an

awesome seasonal drink, and lucky for us, now was the season!

"You were totally right," I told Marley as we stood by the counter and waited for our drinks.

I don't know what she thought I meant, but she liked compliments. Her grin grew almost as big as her hair. Just kidding. That's impossible.

I went on. "I'm going to convince JJ to quit working on Cupid Cards. I've just gotta do it fast, because there are only thirteen—wait, *twelve* days before Valentine's Day."

"I never said you should do that." Marley's smile faded. "When would I have said that? Mrs. Choi was pretty clear, Suki. You're supposed to work together. Even if it stinks, that's what Mrs. Choi said. Besides, don't you need help?" She groaned. "I thought you were agreeing that you were acting like a baby."

I snorted. "Don't get on his side, Mar," I said. Maybe I had dreamed that she said, "Get him to quit," but even if it was just a dream, it was great advice. And, being my best friend, she *should* have said it, so . . . I was going with the plan.

"You really are a baby," she said, and this time I

felt the dig. I didn't like that JJ was coming between us—again.

Marley wrinkled her forehead. She tipped her head toward the front of the shop. "Look who's coming."

The shop was a small place with just a few tables and a counter to buy drinks and snacks. Through the front glass door, I could see JJ coming in with Olivia.

"Hey." Olivia walked over to us. She was wearing workout pants and long-sleeved t-shirt, no coat. The sun was out, but it was still pretty cold, so I figured she must be going to soccer practice soon. Like JJ, Olivia played soccer pretty seriously. They were both on club teams. "Thanks for your help yesterday," Olivia said, more to me than Marley. "Luna needs training. My mom called the local shelter, and there's a puppy class that meets twice a week. I already signed up."

I was immediately overcome with jealousy. How come Olivia, who knew nothing about dogs, got to have a puppy, and I didn't? It was one of those hugely unfair things in the world.

"Great," I said, not really even trying to sound happy.

"I'm getting a new dog, too," JJ said, tugging the zipper on his jacket. "After seeing how cute Olivia's dog was this past weekend, my mom agreed we could get one. I went to the shelter and picked a puppy out. Mom promised to pick her up today."

Hearing that, I had nothing nice to say, so I pinched my lips together.

Olivia asked, "Did you decide what you're going to name her?"

"Sandy," JJ said.

Marley's eyes went wide. I swear she was about to sing, "Tomorrow, tomorrow, I love ya, tomorrow . . ."

"For *Annie*?" Olivia asked. I wished we weren't standing there while they had this conversation, but there was nowhere to go.

"Actually, it's for the beach," JJ told her. "I like to go surfing when we go on vacation. And getting all . . ."

"Sandy!" Olivia finished. They both laughed.

I don't know about Marley, but I felt awkward and oddly left out.

Olivia raised a hand to smooth down her tight bun hairdo and told JJ, "We'd better order."

JJ leaned in toward me on his way to the counter. "You can't avoid me forever." I knew he was taunting me.

"I think I can," I said. JJ was leaning in so close,

it made me nervous. I could hear my charm bracelet jingle.

"The cards won't sell themselves," he said as my name was called from the pickup area.

"I'll take care of everything," I muttered as I pulled back and turned away.

He heard me. "Really? Okay, is that how you want to play?" I recognized the competitive tone in his voice. "Are you sure?"

I was feeling grumpy so I looked him straight in the eye and hissed, "It's science fair all over again."

"If that's what you want . . ." he threatened.

We locked gazes for a stare-down. No one blinked.

Marley grabbed my arm to pull me away, but I was already swept up in the memory.

It was during fourth grade that the besties broke up. Before science fair, Olivia, JJ, Marley and me were so tight, we did everything together. Olivia and JJ were even "dating"—but the fourth-grade version of that just meant that when we all hung out together as usual, they sat next to each other.

JJ and I had teamed up to be partners for the school science fair. Marley and Olivia were another team.

Together, JJ and I came up with a great idea for a

robotic car, and we were supposed to meet up to work on it. I'd spent all week telling him my cool ideas for it.

The day before the project was due, we decided to get together at the library to build the car. He had the parts. I had the plans. But, when I got to the library workroom, he proudly announced that he'd already done it all without me!

The meanest part was when he told me he worked better *alone*, so I'd have to do my own project separately.

I didn't understand how he could leave me hanging like that. We were friends! And partners! Anger had bubbled up in me and spilled over. Without asking why he'd decided to work alone, I raised my voice way too loud for the library, shouting "I work better alone, too!" and slammed the door as I left, clomping home through the park. That day, I didn't even stop at the dog park. I just stomped right by it.

On my way, JJ and his mom drove past me, and JJ called calmly out the window, "See you tomorrow, Suki." The project was due the next morning, and I had no time to do something as cool as the car we'd planned. I whipped up a crappy cardboard volcano, just like about half of the rest of the kids at school did.

I've never been so mad in my whole life.

When Olivia heard what happened, she announced that she supported JJ's decision to work alone. I knew that she and JJ were "boyfriend" and "girlfriend" back then, but didn't really think she'd pick him in the fight. It was fourth grade, not like they were getting married. The way she acted was shocking.

At the time, my last remaining bestie, Marley, backed me up. She and Olivia finished their project together, but never hung out since.

My ex-friend and partner, JJ, won first place at the science fair. Olivia and JJ broke up after that, but stayed really good friends. Now, Olivia was still JJ's friend and Marley was still mine. That was that. (And, honestly, this is why I don't want a boyfriend. When things are going good, dating boys just messes it all up. Why would she have picked him over me and Marley? Boys are what-ever, girl friends are for-ever.)

Before the science fair memory faded completely, I grabbed my drink from the barista a little too fast, and some hot liquid splashed over the edge onto my hand.

"Ouch!" I exclaimed.

"Are you okay?" Marley asked me, concerned. She was more careful in collecting her own cup.

"I'm fine," I insisted, licking the drips off my wrist. I pushed aside my anger. "Can we go to the park instead of hanging out here?" I was desperate to get out of there.

Marley didn't even look back at Olivia and JJ when she said, "Sure. Let's drop our bookbags at my house and I'll get a ball. We can play soccer." Back in the day, we used to go with JJ and Olivia to play soccer in the park all the time.

As we passed, JJ said, "Bye," to us both and then, just to me, sneered, "I work better *alone*, anyway."

Whoa! I knew what that meant! The gauntlet had been thrown down. It was clear what had just happened. JJ was going rogue. Him versus me. Whoever sold the most cards won.

Fine. I was in for the battle.

May the best Cupid *Cards* project win.

Even Cinnamon Bun Swirl with extra whipped cream couldn't shake my rotten mood.

"I hate him," I assured Marley as we set our drinks on the ground next to a small cement bench. She sat on the bench to tie her tennis shoes tighter. I sat on the ground, by the drinks, to stretch. "He thinks all this is funny."

"Do you remember when he won that blue science fair ribbon?" Marley said, not knowing I'd been obsessing about it since the coffee shop. "You were so mad your skin practically turned a matching shade!"

"Yeah, I remember," I said, reaching for my toes. "And I also remember how embarrassing it was for me to have my dad call the teacher at home on a Sunday so I could get permission to do the project by myself." The teacher seemed to already know that JJ had deserted me and was nice about it. I thought that ditching me should have hurt his chance of winning, but it didn't. His mom wasn't mayor back then, so I couldn't even complain that he had an unfair advantage.

"You were really hurt," Marley said. I could feel the echo of that pain in my bones. Clearly, so could she.

"*Bah,*" I said, shaking my shoulders to let the tension slide off. "It doesn't matter. This time, I'm not giving him any of my ideas. Let's see what he can do all on his own. JJ just lobbed the first bomb for a new battle. I'm going to war."

Marley moaned and I thought she was going to call me immature again, but instead she sighed and said, "Okay, I'll help you with the cards."

She was officially still on my side.

Then Marley jumped up and shouted, "Come on, let's play!" and ran out to the middle of the long grassy area. I took one last sip of my drink and felt my mood lift as I joined her on the field. It was chilly, but felt good to be moving.

We kicked the ball back and forth a couple times, and were just getting into a rhythm when Marley gave the ball a strong pump with the inside of her foot. I dove, but the ball bounced over my head, toward the bench.

We both turned to see where it would land.

"Hey!" Marley suddenly shouted. "Get away from there!"

It took me a second to realize she wasn't yelling at me.

The ball stopped in a dirt patch next to where we'd left our drinks. And by our drinks, there was a small puppy! She was golden, maybe some kind of poodle mix, with short curly hair. Her face had white patches on the nose and down her belly. The dog was about the size of two pillows stacked up.

This was the cutest puppy I'd ever seen! And I'd seen a lot of dogs—on the Internet, and from a distance, but still . . .

I asked Marley to quiet down. The puppy had knocked over my drink and was licking up whipped cream and cinnamon off the ground. That probably wasn't very good for her, but I didn't know for sure and I didn't want her to run away, so I told Marley, "Let her have it. I don't want to scare her."

I was amazed the puppy wasn't afraid of us. She stayed where she was and let us move in closer.

"That dog loves Cinnamon Bun Swirl," I said with a giggle.

My mom always warned me about petting strange dogs. This puppy looked super friendly, but how would I know? And did she have all her shots? Those would be mom-like questions. I had no clue about the answers.

I leaned in toward the dog, without touching her, and reported, "She doesn't have a collar. Hmmm . . ."

"Do you think she's stray?" Marley asked me. The two of us were inching closer and closer. I was so close that I could grab the puppy. Suddenly, I stepped on a twig. It snapped. The cracking sound was loud.

The dog looked up, but without any fear in her eyes. She stared at us calmly, then went back to licking my drink off the ground.

"Probably lost. Not stray," I reported. "Her fur isn't matted. And she looks healthy." I studied her more intensely. "I wonder if she has a microchip with her owner's information on it." I'd read that a lot of dog owners did that. They put a small computer chip under the dog's skin. It had information in case the dog got lost. "We'd need to take her to the dog shelter or a vet to get the chip scanned," I said. "They'd find the owner."

"We should do that," Marley said after looking around the park. "I don't see anyone out here looking for a dog."

I glanced around, too. There were a few kids on the playground. A runner dashed by. It was pretty cold for hanging out outside for long. Marley and I were both wearing warm jackets and long pants.

"Let's grab her," Marley said, and before I could remind her that dogs run away when they're being chased, she dove forward.

The puppy took off running, but it didn't seem like she was scared. It was more like she wanted to play. In fact, she ran around me and over to where our soccer ball was lying. The puppy knocked the ball with her nose.

"Oh, that's so adorable," I gushed. "She wants to play soccer." I had a genius idea. "We can wear her out, then when she's tired, we'll pick her up and carry her to the animal shelter. I don't think it's far. Easy peasy."

I picked up the ball. The dog sat down in the grass.

"Okay, Cinnamon Bun," I said. "Let's play!"

"Cinnamon Bun?" Marley squealed. "That's the cutest name ever!"

"It fits," I said with a grin. Inside my heart, I was beginning to hope that this dog had no owner. No chip. And that maybe, if dreams could come true, I'd be able to keep her forever.

I kicked the ball toward Cinnamon Bun. She knocked it back to me with her nose.

Marley chased the ball and pushed it back to me. I shoved it hard with my foot, and this time, Cinnamon jumped up to stop it with her front legs.

"Look at that!" I shouted. "She's great at soccer!"

"Kick the ball to me," Marley called out. I did and Cinnamon Bun pushed it back my way. Before long, she was exhausted and lay down in the grass with her tongue hanging out.

I edged in closer, like I'd seen in those Dog-Talker videos when the trainer didn't want to scare the puppy.

She looked up at me and tipped her head, as if begging for a scratch. Putting my fears of touching a stray aside, I sat down in the grass and scooted in closer. She met me halfway and put her head in my lap. I was wearing thin gloves, and I took them off so I could feel how soft her fur was. When I ran my hand across her back, I could feel that it was like cotton.

I laughed out loud. "She's so soft!" I exclaimed. "And she wants me to scratch her neck." Cinnamon was shoving her head under my hand, directing my fingers.

"Don't just pet her—you gotta catch her," Marley said, coming forward and standing over me. "We have to take her to the shelter."

I swear Cinnamon Bun understood that last bit, because before Marley even finished the word "shelter," the dog yanked her head away from my hand and leapt up. In a tornado of fur and feet, she ran past

Marley and into a thick row of bushes at the back of the park.

I paused, half-expecting her to come right back. I mean she liked me, right? Didn't she want to be mine forever? We could work it out!

When a few long minutes went by and Cinnamon Bun didn't return, I started to worry.

"Where'd she go?" I asked Marley, as if she'd know.

Marley simply shrugged.

We rushed to the bushes. There was a thick hedge that separated the border of the park from the apartment complex behind it.

I called out dog training commands. "Here, Cinnamon Bun! Come, Cinnamon Bun." But she didn't come. She probably wasn't trained for that yet. Maybe someday I could train her in those classes that Olivia was talking about!

Marley jogged around to where there was a break in the bushes and a path to the apartments. She looked around there while I looked under the bushes where I'd last seen Cinnamon Bun, in case she was hiding.

There was no sign of the puppy anywhere. And it was going to start getting dark soon.

I stood up and Marley came back.

"What are we going to do?" she asked. "She's out there in the big world, all alone."

It was dramatic, but true.

"I think . . ." I said, pausing to consider possibilities. "We have to come back tomorrow with another drink."

I crossed my fingers. If Cinnamon Bun really liked the Cinnamon Bun Swirl, I hoped she'd be back for more.

Chapter Four
A BAD DAY

Still Tuesday, February 1

"Mom! Dad!" I entered the house, slammed the door behind me, and kicked off my shoes in one speedy move.

"Breathe, baby. Slow it down," my mom said, coming around the corner into the hallway. My mom used to be an accountant, but last year, when her back started hurting from sitting all day, she discovered yoga. For her, it was not just a new job—it changed her life. Everything became about the yoga way of life, and she was always trying to get me and my dad into it, too. Last Christmas I got two different *Namaste* sweatshirts and my own sticky mat. My dad got foam stability blocks and a stinky detox eye pillow.

For a woman whose head was going to explode every April at tax season, she was now the most mellow human being on earth. And her back never hurt anymore.

"Is Dad here?" I wanted to tell them both about the dog in the park. Maybe we could go back before it was totally dark and try to find her.

"He's working late," Mom said. She wasn't super skinny from all that yoga, but she was super healthy. I thought she looked nice in her leggings and sweater. I told her that.

"Thanks," Mom replied. "You're full of compliments tonight, eh, Suki? What do you want?"

"I wasn't complimenting you for a reason," I said, adding, "but your hair does look good today. Did you do something special?"

She ran a hand over her tight black ponytail and said, "Out with it."

"Oh, fine. Promise you won't say no before you hear the whole story?" Together we moved into the living room and sat on the couch.

Mom squinted at me. "I promise. Now, before you

tell me how pretty my brown eyes are, what's up?" She leaned back into the couch.

One thing that was better when Mom was an accountant was that she didn't listen very well, so back then I might have gotten her to agree to a dog simply by confusing her while she finished an email. I'd have tried to slip it into a list, like: sign this permission slip, can I have a dog, open this jar . . . It sometimes worked.

This New Mom pinned me with those pretty brown eyes and said, "Go on, Suki. What is it that you want?"

I sighed. "Same thing I always want."

"A dog?" She began to shake her head.

I held up a hand. "You promised to hear the whole story."

Got her. Mom's word is her bond. "Okay," she said, resigning to it. "I'm listening."

I told her about Cinnamon Bun and how worried I was that she was out in the park alone. "We've gotta go find her," I said. "Tonight." I stood up and grabbed her hand. "Now."

"I don't think—" Mom started, when Dad walked in. He was tall and thin with gray streaks in his hair. Dad was also awkwardly pale from working inside all the time—even when he traveled for work, he was still inside all the time. He looked a lot like a guy who'd never seen sunlight.

"What's going on, Pumpkin?" That's what he called me, even though I was way too old for a nickname.

"I—" I was going to have him make the same promise, then explain, but Mom cut in.

"Suki and Marley found a stray dog in the park. She wants to go rescue it," she said.

Dad lowered his nerd glasses and stared at me over the rims. "You know where we stand on dogs," he said.

"But Cinnamon Bun needs us," I said, my voice sounding a little more whiny than I meant it to.

"I'm sorry, Pumpkin." Dad shook his head, which made the gray streaks in his brown hair glisten. "No dogs. You can't take care of one, and Mom and I are too busy."

Mom gave my hand a sympathetic squeeze and said she agreed with Dad.

"But she's all alone in the park!" My voice rose. "Please!"

"I'll call the animal shelter," Dad said. "I'll let them know you saw a stray in the park and they'll go find her. She can stay at the shelter."

That sounded terrible. The shelter was noisy, with rows and rows of sad dogs in cages, hoping for a family. Well, I imagined it was. I'd never actually been there, but that was what shelters looked like on TV.

"Poor Cinnamon Bun," I said with a long sigh.

Mom and Dad moved into the kitchen.

"I'll set out dinner," Mom told me, blowing a kiss as she left the room.

"I'll arrange a dogcatcher," Dad said, taking his cell phone from his pocket.

I flopped back into our cushy couch and sighed again. "And I'll just sit here with my crushed dreams," I muttered tragically, "Poor, poor Cinnamon Bun."

"Any news on Cinnamon Bun?" Marley asked while opening her locker the next morning at school.

I'd texted Marley to fill her in on the situation last night before bed. She'd replied by texting *This doggy dream is a foggy dream*. And, of course, she called a minute later to sing that line to me.

Marley shoved her jacket inside her locker, then started going through a stack of mixed-up papers to find her homework.

"I called the shelter this morning before school,"

I told her, looking away from her mess. "They never found Cinnamon Bun."

"That's good, right?" Marley said. "You didn't want her trapped, crying in a sad cage."

"Yeah, but I also don't want her alone on the street," I said.

Marley found what she needed and closed her locker door. "You're confusing," she told me.

"I know," I agreed. I opened my locker, which was next to Marley's, and stuck an unmarked bright red binder inside. It was the to-do list from last year's Cupid Cards, plus other important notes. I'd saved everything we'd tried and had written down what worked and what didn't. I was planning to crack into it during my free time. I'd been distracted the day before, but I had to get started ASAP. And that meant today.

As Marley and I walked to class, I saw Olivia standing by JJ's locker. He gave me a wink and smile. That was suspicious! What was he up to? I was curious, and at the same time, I didn't want to know.

After school, Marley and I went back to the park. We had fresh Cinnamon Bun Swirl drinks, plus I'd stopped at the market and bought a box of dog treats and a leash.

"We have to find her," I declared. I set our drinks on the nearest bench, the same one where we'd started the day before. It was sunny but colder today, so we didn't bring the soccer ball. I was wearing my thin gloves and a light scarf. We both sat down.

Marley poured some of her drink on the grass and we waited to see if the dog would show up to lap it up.

We waited, shivering, as the coffee drink soaked into the ground and the whipped cream faded away.

I looked toward the bushes where Cinnamon Bun had disappeared yesterday.

"Stay with the drinks, just in case she shows up," I told Marley. Then I ran to the bushes and made a trail of dog treats from there back to Marley.

We waited.

And waited.

After an hour of hanging around and getting colder and colder, Marley announced, "It's time to go, Suki." She stood up and began air-drumming. "I have to practice tonight. I'm learning a song to play at my dad's birthday party and don't want my fingers to fall off."

I rolled my eyes. Her dad's birthday was in eight months.

Marley grabbed her empty cup and turned to me. "Are you coming?"

I looked out over the trail of dog treats and said, "I think I'll stay a little longer."

Marley laughed and rolled her eyes at me. "Don't let *your* fingers fall off!"

I wiggled them. "Not even cold," I lied.

I hung out for about another half an hour before my nose was red and running. I knew I couldn't stay there much longer, watching the bushes for a dog that I was pretty sure wasn't coming.

And then, just as I was about to give up, I saw her.

First, it was just a flash of golden fur, and then the whole puppy! Cinnamon Bun came out of the bushes and onto the lawn. Then she looked at me, I swear she did, before immediately turning around to go back the way she came.

Clutching my drink, I jumped up off the bench and ran toward the bushes as fast as I could. Bits of now-cold Swirl dribbled out the lid and onto my hand as I bounced.

The bushes looked longer and thicker than ever

before. I had to find the way through to the other side, but in my desperation, I couldn't recall where exactly I needed to go. When I finally found a pathway, Cinnamon Bun was gone.

I cursed myself for taking so long. Maybe, like Cinnamon, I should have tried to go under the prickly hedge. I might have gotten stuck, but at least I would know which way she'd gone!

"Cinnamon! Cinnamon Bun!" I called her name a few times before foolishly realizing that it was just the name I'd given her, so she didn't know it. Then I picked a direction and ran to the corner, looking around frantically. In the dimming afternoon light, I searched for another golden flash.

When I didn't see anything, I dashed back to the bushes. There was a little bit of drink still left in my cup, so I dumped the contents onto the sidewalk and then tried to waft the scent in every direction by waving my arms over it. Maybe Cinnamon Bun would smell the yumminess and come back.

If anyone saw me, they would think I'd gone crazy. I was standing in a puddle of spilled drink waving my hands like a bird about to take flight.

Yep. Of course the moment I was swooping my

hands like a circus mime was when JJ suddenly appeared. "What are you doing?" he asked with a chuckle.

"I—" Drat. "Science project," I lied. "I'm measuring wind speeds . . . Since there's no wind this afternoon, I was making some with my hands."

He stared at me. "I'm in your science class," he said. "Must have missed that assignment."

Whoops. I didn't know what to say to that. "It's e-extra credit," I stammered. "I asked Mr. Gibbons for extra homework." That sounded lame. Who asked for more work?

"Good thing I don't need extra credit, then," JJ bragged. After that, thankfully, he changed the subject.

Too late, I realized I should have told him it was a new workout and then jogged away. Because what he wanted to talk about next was the Cupid Cards.

"Still not interested in working together on the Cupid Cards?" he asked, emphasizing the word *Cards*. Um, what? *He* was the one who suggested we go our separate ways in the first place!

"It *is* a lot of work." JJ tipped his head as if thoughts were just now coming into his brain. "I'm thinking

I need volunteers to sell cards. Plus, I need to get the candy. And red paper. And then more volunteers to cut them into heart-shaped cards and tape on the lollipops. And then, after they are sold, I'll need more volunteers to sort the cards for classrooms and deliver them." JJ raised a finger for each item on that list and then wiggled them all at me. "Is that all?"

I looked at him in shock. That actually *was* everything that needed to be done. Had he somehow seen my to-do list? I hadn't had time to look at it in school, so I had it in my bookbag now. It had been locked up all day. Totally secure. There was no way he could've seen it.

Truth was, I didn't really need the binder anyway. I had it all memorized.

After hearing JJ's list, I didn't tell him that, last year, we'd realized that it saved time if you let people choose their candy when they bought the cards, and just taped it on then. I kept my mouth closed. I wasn't going to help!

JJ touched my arm and added, "And if I'm going to sell more cards this year, I'll need to start selling them early."

I squinted down at his hand and he quickly removed it. Reminding myself that the goal was still to scare him away, I said, "You're missing a lot of steps." It wasn't true.

"Sure," he said sarcastically. And with a sinister smile, he added, "I was just making sure I knew everything and wasn't missing anything that had to be done. So . . ." he turned to leave. "Thanks for confirming it, Suki."

He'd used me! Just like he had for the science project! I'd somehow told him everything he needed to get done without even saying anything. Blast him!

"Good luck with your science project," JJ said, taking a few large steps down the path.

"What?" I'd forgotten that was what I told him I was doing. "Oh, right." I started waving my hands again. "Almost done here."

He nodded to himself and I swore it looked like he was holding back laughter.

"If you get too cold, we just moved into these apartments." He pointed. "Third building to the left." With that, JJ walked away.

As soon as he was out of sight, I dropped my arms stiffly to my side.

This was embarrassing! And disappointing.

JJ was apparently already working on the Cupid Cards project, which I hadn't started.

Cinnamon Bun had disappeared.

Could the day get any worse?

Chapter Five
A HAPPY PLACE

Wednesday, February 2, right after the disaster at the park

I muttered to myself the whole way home.

"It didn't make sense that he knew everything on my to-do list for the Cupid Cards!" I didn't want to accept that he was just smart and could've figured it out on his own.

This was serious business, and JJ was so casual about it. He made me mad.

I was so busy trying to figure out if JJ had come up with the to-do list on his own, or if someone from last year had clued him in, that I forgot to turn at my street! Next thing I knew, I'd gone three blocks out of my way. When I looked up, I was standing in front of the animal shelter.

I'd only ever seen the outside of the long building. Of course, I often imagined what it was like inside, from commercials on TV of pathetic animals desperate to be adopted. My parents were so stubborn. If I faced reality, I'd admit that I'd never get to adopt a dog. I started to turn away, then stopped.

Wait. What if the reason I couldn't find Cinnamon Bun was that the dogcatcher had already gotten her? Funny, now that I was thinking about it, I'd never seen a dogcatcher except on TV. Was it even a real job? Anyway, if they did get Cinnamon Bun, where was she now? What was she doing?

There was only one way to find out the answers to all my questions. I pushed open the glass door to the shelter and went inside.

I had to go through two gates to get to the front office. I understood that the system was so if a dog got loose and one gate was open, it still couldn't run away.

Once inside, there was a lobby area, sort of like in an office building, but behind the long, tall counter, leashes, carriers, bowls, and pet treats were for sale.

There was everything someone might need to get their new pet home.

"Hi," I said to the woman at the counter. She had short, smooth brown hair and a name tag that said *Louisa*. I guessed she was about the same age as my parents, but not nearly as fit as my mom and not pale like my dad. This woman obviously went outside sometimes.

"How can I help you?" she asked, peering over wire-rimmed glasses at me. "Are you here for the puppy training class?" Louisa pointed to a long hall-way to my left. "The classroom is that way."

I stepped back so she could see that I didn't have a dog with me.

"Oh," Louisa said, "I thought maybe you were with the other girl who just came in. She was about your age."

"That was probably Olivia," I said, remembering she'd said something about training for Luna. Her class must have started this afternoon. "I'm Suki."

"Nice to meet you." She was staring suspiciously at me now. "Are you interested in pet adoption?" she asked. "We have cats and dogs and the cutest bunny that came in today."

"Oh!" A bunny sounded awesome. Maybe if my parents rejected the dog idea again, I'd try for that bunny instead.

I told myself to focus. "No. No pets," I said, adding softly, "Not today." Then louder, "There's a stray dog out in the neighborhood. I was wondering if maybe the dogcatcher found her."

"We don't have anyone with that job title," Louisa explained. She pushed some papers to the side, tucking them behind her computer screen, and gave me her full attention. "We call them animal control officers now. But they don't usually drive around looking for strays. Most stray dogs are brought here by people who find them, because it's safer to put them here than leave them on the street. We have a volunteer vet check them out. Plus, there's the hope the animals will get adopted."

I liked that. It sounded positive. But, then again, I didn't want Cinnamon Bun to get adopted by anyone but me.

I asked, "Did you get a small gold-colored dog in this afternoon?" I explained that I'd seen Cinnamon Bun in the park, but she had run away.

Louisa typed something into a computer on the

desk and then shook her head. "It doesn't look like it." She pointed to the area behind her. "But if you want to go peek at the dogs, maybe you'll find her."

"Really? Can I?" I hadn't been expecting to be able to go back to the area where the dogs were kept. Part of me was nervous that it was going to be so sad to see all those dogs in cages. But another part of me was super excited to see if Cinnamon Bun was there!

"If you want to adopt, your whole family has to come, but if you're just looking to see if a specific stray is here, I can help. Come on. Let's look," Louisa said. She shouted into another room, and a boy I knew from school, Ben Ryan, popped his head out. Ben was a year older than me. I didn't know he volunteered at the shelter.

"Yeah, Mom?" he said. Ben was twirling a pencil in one hand and holding a calculator in the other.

"Watch the desk, please," she said. "I'm taking Suki to see the dogs."

"Adopting?" Ben asked me.

"Nah." I really wished I was there to adopt. "I saw a stray in the park and was checking if she's here."

He gave me a thumbs-up. "Gotcha. I hate it when dogs are out on the street at night." He raised his bushy eyebrows at me. "There are coyotes that prowl the neighborhood in the dark, looking for a tasty dinner. Little dogs are like popcorn to coyotes."

"Benny!" His mother pointed a finger at him. "Don't scare her."

"It's true," Ben argued. He looked even harder at me. "Trust me, I hang out here nearly every afternoon. There are horror stories to tell . . ."

I grimaced. "Yuck." I wasn't sure whether to believe him, but a chill ran down my spine, thinking about Cinnamon Bun out alone.

"Stop it!" Louisa—Mrs. Ryan, as I was now thinking of her—told Ben. "There's no reason to put bad thoughts in Suki's head. If the dog she found isn't here, maybe it'll come in tonight or tomorrow."

"Fingers crossed," Ben said with a sinister chuckle. "The cute ones make the most delicious snacks."

"Ignore him," Mrs. Ryan told me. "He's just teasing."

"Maybe I'm teasing," Ben called after us as we walked toward the back door to the place the dogs were kept. "Or maybe I'm not." I glanced back at him and he snapped his jaw like a coyote.

"I think Ben is good for business," I told her as she reached up to open the door. "I'd rather adopt all the dogs in the shelter than let them get eaten by wolves."

"I suppose he has his strengths." She chuckled lightly and smiled. "Well, let's see if your stray is here."

We passed through a thick door to the back area. Excitement rolled through me. The room was partitioned into two large areas; one was marked with a big sign that said CATS and another marked DOGS. The whole room smelled clean, like bleach and fresh flowery shampoo. When I took a deeper breath, I sensed there was a pet smell, too, but it wasn't stinky or gross. I liked it.

While Mrs. Ryan stopped and filled out a form that was lying on a long counter where food bowls were stacked, I closed my eyes and listened to the dogs barking. There were deep growls and high yelps. Short bursts and long stretched-out howls. Toward the back of the big room, I could also hear cats meowing. I squeezed my eyes tighter as I took it all in.

Marley loved her songs, but this was true music to me.

When I opened my eyes again, I let the loud yelping sounds fade to the back of my mind and focused on seeing the animals.

The shelter wasn't anything like the sad places on TV.

It was wonderful.

We walked toward the dogs. They were paired up in cages, but the cages were big and roomy and all had little doorways to the outside, where there was additional caged space for animals to hang out and get fresh air.

I walked up to a cage where the saddest dog with big brown eyes looked out from between the bars. He was a large mutt with a massive amount of black fur. I bet he weighed almost as much as me. He sighed a long sorry sound, and didn't stand up.

"That's Bowzer," Mrs. Ryan told me. "He's a Briard mix and has been here almost a whole year." She pointed at a sign on the wall that said OUR LONGEST RESIDENT and had a photo of Bowzer taped below it.

That explained his depressed, drooping face.

"His family was moving to England and couldn't take him along, so they left him here," Mrs. Ryan said. She grabbed a meaty chew treat from a dish high on the cage door and held it out to Bowzer through the cage's metal slits.

He dragged himself up and lumbered toward us. With a long pink tongue, Bowzer scooped the treat from Mrs. Ryan's hand, gobbled it down, then slunk back onto the floor. He looked like a brown fuzzy carpet.

"Why hasn't he been adopted?" I asked. I could feel my heart rate pick up. This adopting-a-dog thing could be a big problem for me. I wanted Cinnamon Bun to live with me, but I also wanted to take care of all these dogs.

"I think he was a good dog when his owners lived here, but since they left, he's had issues," she said. "Bowzer isn't nice to the prospective families. Or other dogs. Or cats. That makes it hard to find him a home."

"I bet he's just grumpy since he got left behind," I said. "Can I give him a treat?"

"He's okay with the staff here because he knows us," she said. "I don't mind testing him out with a stranger, but please be careful. Let's see how he does."

She handed me a treat and I held it out, placing my fingers and the treat just slightly through the cage bars.

Bowzer didn't move slowly like before. He lunged off the floor, snarling, his sharp teeth flashing.

"Oh!" I gasped. I dropped the treat into the cage and pulled back my fingers faster than I think I'd ever moved before, and stepped way, way back from the cage. Bowzer snarfed the treat off the floor and settled back down as if nothing odd had happened.

"Sorry about that," Mrs. Ryan told me, looking at the dog, who once again seemed comatose on the floor. "Are you okay, Suki?"

"I'm fine," I assured her. A little scared, but fine. I blinked hard, taking a moment to calm down.

Mrs. Ryan gave a stern look at Bowzer. "No!" she said firmly. He glared at her with an expression that said, "What? I didn't do anything."

"Other shelters probably wouldn't have kept him," Mrs. Ryan told me as we moved away. "He can't be caged with another dog and, obviously, he's unpredictable. But we pride ourselves on being a no-kill shelter."

I knew what that meant. Some animal shelters didn't have space for animals that couldn't be adopted, and it made me feel heartbroken. Now that I'd seen Bowzer in action, I was sure he wasn't going to a family. He'd eat kids for dinner. But another shelter might not have let him hang around so long that his picture was on the board. I bet that some other shelters didn't even have a board.

"Our shelter is committed to keeping the animals

that come in here until we find a home for each one."
Mrs. Ryan turned her back on Bowzer's cage. "Even if
that means they stay here forever."

"Poor Bowzer," I said with a frown. Sure, he scared
me nearly to death, but I felt bad for the brute.

"He's okay," Mrs. Ryan told me. "Bowzer knows he
can stay here as long as he wants." Taking my arm,
she led me toward a cage a few doors down where
happy puppies barked as we approached.

"We found this litter under a bridge by the high-
way yesterday." She pointed at their little yellow bobbing heads.

I quickly counted six babies.

"They were abandoned." Seeing my face, she
assured me, "Don't worry. Puppies get adopted fast."

I nodded. "Of course they do." If I were picking a
dog today, I'd want one of these puppies, too. They
were bouncy and playful and mega-cute.

"Not every shelter is as compassionate as ours," Mrs.
Ryan told me as we reached the end of the long row of
cages. "Did you see the dog you were looking for?"

"No," I said, frowning. "She's not here." I added a
hopeful "Yet," because I knew this shelter was a special place.

I'd have to check every day until she was brought in. Then I'd ask my parents . . . again. Maybe, if they came here, they'd see how much these dogs need homes. Our house would be a great home!

That gave me an amazing idea.

"Mrs. Ryan, do you take volunteers?" I asked. This way, I would already be here when Cinnamon Bun arrived.

I held my breath while she answered.

"Yes," she told me. "Volunteers have to be twelve years old and like working with animals."

"I know just the person." I let out a long breath and smiled, pointing at myself. "When can I start?"

I made it home in record time.

There were a lot of things I needed to do, but I couldn't think about anything other than working at the shelter. Mrs. Ryan said I could start immediately. Tomorrow!

I'd begin with the easy stuff like walking dogs and cleaning up poop. Poop duty sounded great. I'd do anything to be there.

I burst into my house.

"Mom! Dad!"

"Can't you come in slowly? Mindfully?" my mother asked. "You're going to break the door."

I glanced back at the front door. It was solid wood.

Mindful. That was a mom-word, meaning I needed to think more about . . . well, everything. Less slamming, more thinking about the door. *Sheesh.* The door didn't have feelings!

"Can I volunteer at the animal shelter after school?" I blurted, the words rushing out of my mouth like a train through a tunnel.

"Sure," Mom said without hesitation. "Is that where you've been all afternoon?"

I realized that hours had passed since school let out. Lucky for me, Mom wasn't a helicopter-worrier, plus I could see that she was proud I'd come home with such a "productive" idea. She added, "But only if you keep your grades up."

"I will!" I said. "I promise!"

"And take care of commitments you've already made to the student council."

"On it," I agreed eagerly. I already had my list of what I needed to do for the Cupid Cards.

"And don't bring home any of the strays," she said. "No sneaking a puppy home in your coat."

I hadn't actually thought of that, but it was a pretty good idea. When I found Cinnamon Bun, I could keep her in my closet. Mom and Dad would never know.

"Suki!" Mom said, as if reading my thoughts. First JJ, now her. I was going to have to stop thinking so loudly.

"Okay, okay," I promised. "There was no way that was going to work anyway. My closet's really small and overstuffed already."

"Fine, and one more thing," she said, putting her hands on her hips.

I waited for it.

"You must be home in the evenings for dinner," she told me. "It's family time."

Yeah, yeah. Already counted on that rule. It was the reason Mom didn't worry where I was after school.

"Deal!" I shouted, then gave mom a fast, tight hug. "Thanks!" I shouted, kicking off my shoes and skipping upstairs to video chat with Marley.

For the next few hours, talking about the shelter was all I could do. Even Marley grew bored listening. I talked forever over dinner to Dad until he asked me if anything else happened at school. I even called Grandma in Florida. Then I rushed through all the homework I'd been ignoring all evening. Talking about the shelter was way more exciting!

Then, because I was so jazzed up and couldn't sleep, I used leftover red paper from last year and cut out little red hearts for Cupid Cards until my fingers hurt. I bet JJ hadn't started doing *that*!

That night, when I fell asleep, I was happier than ever!

chapter six
DESPERATE MEASURES

Thursday, February 3

"Rotem and I are working on a way to find and trap Cinnamon Bun," Marley told me as we slid our hot-lunch trays on the long tables that filled the school's multipurpose room.

Marley and Rotem Arons were good friends. He wrote songs and played bass in Marley's band. The thing about Rotem was that he was also the smartest kid at school. He was younger than us but had also skipped a year, so he was already in eighth-grade classes. It was hard to believe he'd start high school next year, leaving me and Marley behind in middle school.

Rotem took a bite of his hamburger, then grabbed a notebook from his backpack. The cover had a lock on it and he wore the key on a chain around his neck.

"This is where I keep my best ideas," he told me. "I don't want anyone to know what I'm working on." His dark, curly hair was cut close to his head. "I'm planning to be the youngest to win a Nobel Prize. I just can't decide if it'll be in physics or chemistry."

I waited for him to laugh, or smile, to show he was kidding. He wasn't.

"Why not both?" I suggested.

"I've thought about that as well," he replied seriously.

Then he opened his notebook and shoved the key and chain back inside his shirt. Turning a little away from Marley and me so we couldn't see the pages, he flipped to the middle of the book.

"He keeps song lyrics in there, too," Marley told me. "I don't get to see anything until they are exactly perfect, just the way he wants them." She smiled and whispered, "I've never seen one."

Rotem heard her. "If it's not perfect, it's not happening," he said.

I was worried he'd set himself up for disappointment. Then again, if anyone was going to get things to perfection, it was probably him. As far as I could tell, Rotem was superhuman.

"Mar told me about the dog in the park," Rotem said. "I devised a way to catch her for you."

"That sounds awesome," I said leaning toward him, not just to see the page, but because I knew it freaked him out. Rotem was funny like that. He didn't like anyone to breathe in his space.

Just as I expected, he pulled back away from me, subtly giving me the message to back off. Then, when I was safely in my own air zone, he turned the notebook toward me, careful to pin down the other pages with his thumbs.

Clearing his throat, Rotem said, "This is an obstacle course."

I glanced at Marley. She was nodding softly, hanging on his every word. I wasn't sure if that meant she was following closely or just pretending to while actually bouncing her head to a melody rattling in her brain.

"Okay, I'm with you," I said. "So how do we catch my dog?" I'd started to think of Cinnamon Bun as mine.

"First, we have to lure Cinnamon Bun to us," Marley said. She pointed to Rotem's notebook. "We are going to create a Cinnamon Swirl perimeter." I could tell she was using Rotem's vocabulary and it made me giggle.

"A perimeter?" I asked, raising an eyebrow.

"Yes," Rotem explained. "We drizzle Cinnamon Bun drink around the edges of the park. Then we set treats at very precise intervals." He raised one finger and moved it in a spiral pattern to demonstrate. When he flipped a notebook page, I could see that he had a mathematical chart drawn out. Clearing his throat, Rotem went on. "I used measurements estimated on the size of the dog's legs and how fast we predict she can run. Though not exact, the numbers should be close."

"Nice," I said, looking at the way the treats were set out. If Cinnamon Bun ate one treat, she'd be in smelling distance of the next one. Each treat had a fun task for Cinnamon Bun to do before she reached it, like going under a little tunnel or over a stack of books. The obstacle course spiraled inward to the center of the park.

"In the middle," Marley continued, "is the trap."

Apparently, Rotem could also draw. (Was there

anything he couldn't do?) He'd sketched a detailed box with a gate attached, all covered with leafy camouflage. That was where Cinnamon Bun would get caught.

"Dogs like scratching their backs on leaves," Rotem assured me.

I smiled because I knew that already. We'd probably seen the same Internet videos.

Rotem seemed very certain of himself when he explained, "We're going to build a robot rover that's covered with leaves, so when she scratches herself on the leaves, the robot will move forward slowly, leading her into the cage, where a mechanical arm will hold out a spoon of peanut butter and lure her into the trap."

I bet Marley had told him about the peanut butter trick.

"I'm going to put bumpers on the robot, so it'll softly close the door for us," Rotem said.

"The cage door locks automatically," Marley said with a huge smile. She seemed especially proud when she explained about the bed that would be inside the cage. "It'll be super comfy, and I found a blanket with little cinnamon buns printed on it. We can totally use that!"

This all seemed great, but also really complicated.

"Uh, isn't this a bit much?" I asked them. I had too much to do for the Cupid Cards project to be spending so much time building a trap and robots. I needed to go by the store after school to get the candy for the cards, and to cut more hearts.

"I really don't think we need all this." I pointed to the obstacle course. "It's too difficult."

Rotem studied his diagram, then concluded, "This is the *only* way to catch that dog."

"We're going to build the robot at Rotem's house on Friday night!" Marley cheered.

"I have everything we need," Rotem put in. "My dad owns a hardware store." He finished the last of his burger and chugged his milk. "Gotta run to the science lab!" he said, closing up his book and relocking the lock before grabbing his backpack and taking off.

I wasn't so sure about Rotem's masterful plan. It was way too complicated. Plus, I was desperate to find Cinnamon Bun before Saturday. Otherwise, she'd have two more nights out with coyotes.

I was about to tell Marley my doubts, when she said, "I joined Coding Club."

"Oh, wow! I didn't know you were interested in coding."

She explained, "Rotem told me about how I can use computer programming for music and lights with the band, so I signed up!" We walked together to the trash, with Marley air-drumming while I held our trays.

She was so excited about coding that I considered going to a meeting, too. Maybe I could code something that would help train dogs? That would be cool . . . But first, I needed a dog!

Chapter Seven
HEAT'S ON

Friday, February 4

When I got to school the next morning, JJ was standing near my locker talking to a group of guys from his soccer team. I was pretty sure he was waiting for me, so I went into the bathroom and stayed there till after the bell rang and he was gone. There was no way I'd get tricked into telling him more stuff about how to do the Cupid Cards project.

Between classes, I rushed to the bathroom to make sure he couldn't talk to me.

By the time lunch came around, people were asking if I felt okay. I didn't want to tell them I was just avoiding JJ. Maybe Marley was right and I was acting immature, maybe even like a baby, but I was willing to accept that.

I stalled long enough before lunch that everyone was already in the cafeteria when I walked in.

My plan was to slink in unnoticed. But then, something in the far left corner, over by where the trays were stacked, caught my eye. Instead of a single line of students waiting for their trays, people were clumped up in a big group. I could see some students raising their hands and heard a few cries of, "I'll do it!"

I scanned the room. Usually kids were at every table and the place was buzzing with conversation. Now the tables seemed pretty empty.

I searched for Marley. It was the easiest time I'd ever had finding her. She was with Rotem at a long table. They both had already eaten most of their food and were sitting together poring over something in his Nobel Prize notebook. Probably the plans to catch Cinnamon Bun.

I dashed to them and blurted out, "What's going on?"

Rotem jumped back, nearly bumping heads with Marley as he shot up in surprise to see me there. "I—" He looked at Marley and groaned. "We—"

"Sorry," I laughed, and dropped my backpack on the floor as I sat down next to Marley. "I meant, what's going on in the corner?" I was going to have to go brave the crowd and get a tray soon, since I needed lunch.

Marley raised her eyebrows and squinted at me. "What do you mean?"

I pointed at the group in the back of the room. The crowd seemed to be thinning a little as people got trays and went through the lunch line.

"Uh . . ." Marley looked to Rotem. He stared back, looking worried.

"What?" I was near shouting. "What is it?"

Marley paused for a beat, then came out with a sentence that blew me away. "JJ and Olivia are at a table over there, signing up volunteers to deliver Cupid Cards on Valentine's Day."

"Are you kidding me?" Okay, I kind of yelled that too loud. People turned to look at me. I lowered my voice into a rough hiss. "Olivia's not even on student council! This is all wrong!"

I'd cut hearts out at night by myself. I'd gotten candy. That was what JJ needed to be doing! It wasn't time to get volunteers to deliver the Cupid Cards yet—he hadn't even sold any cards yet. And first, you had to *have* actual paper hearts to sell! If there were going to be volunteers involved right now, they should be for cutting—*only* cutting. Still, JJ was going to end up claiming everyone who would want to volunteer before I even got a chance to find anyone!

I was furious. "I'll be right back," I told Marley and Rotem.

My clunky boots thumped with every step across the white tile lunchroom floor. I could hear each step pounding in my head.

When I reached the back of the crowd, I shoved my way through to get to the table.

There was a big handwritten sign above the table that said MAKE THIS VALENTINE'S DAY BETTER THAN LAST YEAR! SIGN UP TO DELIVER CUPID CARDS HERE. And under that, in small letters, it said SKIP CLASS TO HELP!

That didn't even make sense. Skipping class? Only the student council members could do that. JJ couldn't promise the same deal to everyone.

I pointed at the sign. "What is this?"

"Sign-ups," JJ told me, sounding smug. "Want to help out?"

"You can't just promise everyone that they can skip classes," I sneered. "Only people on student council can, with special permission." I was itching to rip down the stupid sign above his head. "And it's just fourth period, right after lunch, which is the last chance for sales. *Fourth period* is when the cards are delivered." His banner seemed to say that students could pick any class to skip.

"I met with Principal Hollis yesterday after school," JJ said. He was acting like there was nothing weird about that, while Olivia signed up two seventh graders for third period. "Hollis got what I told him. To sell more cards and make more money for the school, we'd need help. He agreed that as long as students stayed on top of their homework, and were actually working on the cards, anyone who wanted could skip a class or two. Like maybe *third period* we might want some kids to help sort cards into delivery boxes. Or *second period*, someone can go around to classes, selling more cards. As you know, there are a lot of things that could be done on Valentine's Day." He picked up a clipboard. "Everyone just has to sign up so we can prove no one's ditching for no good reason. A bunch of guys from the soccer team have already signed on."

Every word that JJ said made my blood boil a little bit more.

"Second period! Third period! What are you talking about?" I was like a volcano, ready to burst. "This *is* science fair all over again!" I exclaimed, leaning against the table and meeting his eyes. Kids around us had stopped to listen. I knew I was making a scene but didn't care. JJ was stealing my project! "For that, you went to the teacher to break up our science group, and now you're going to the principal behind my back!" I shouted.

"I—" JJ started, then stopped abruptly. He was looking over my shoulder.

I turned.

Mrs. Choi was standing there, hands on her hips. "Hi," she said, flat expression. No smile. "Is there a problem?"

I spun around. "JJ went to the principal." I waved my hands wildly. "He set up this table and is asking for volunteers! He said they could skip class. Any class they want. And I'll bet that he hasn't even cut any hearts yet!" My list of complaints was miles long, but she stopped me.

"Suki, let's take a walk," she said calmly. "We're going outside. Do you want a coat?"

I shook my head. The sun was out and my blood was on fire.

"Let's go then," she said, leading the way.

I could feel JJ's dopey smile following me as he went back to signing up volunteers.

Mrs. Choi and I left the lunchroom and went outside. It was chillier than I expected. I wrapped my arms around my waist while my teacher zipped up her puffy jacket.

"JJ came to me yesterday and told me that you've been too busy to co-chair with him."

"That's not true!" I protested. I mean, I'd been working at the shelter—I was even promoted from dog poop cleaner to dog food scooper, but I was working on the Cupid Cards, too. I wasn't just doing one thing. I was, as Mom would say, multitasking. Plus, he was the one who suggested working separately! But I couldn't say that. As far as Mrs. Choi knew, we were working together. I didn't think she'd be happy with our change of plans.

My teacher sat on a bench and motioned for me to sit beside her. "JJ had some things that he said needed to get done right away, so I told him to proceed." I opened my mouth to protest, but she went on. "He had my permission to go to the principal's office."

What was I supposed to say to that? My own teacher had turned against me. Though I guess she hadn't done it on purpose.

I took a breath and let the cool air fill my lungs. This was not what I wanted. This was not what I'd planned!

"JJ gave me a printed copy of a to-do list," Mrs. Choi said. "I assume you saw it?"

"No," I said, but assumed it was a list sort of like he'd told me about at the park. My list.

"Suki." Her voice was low and soft. "As long as the project gets done, I don't really care who does which part. You and JJ are working together on this, so I want you to work it out with him." She stood.

"But, I—"

She gave me a look that shut me down. I couldn't tell her that JJ and I were competing with each other. Not when JJ already seemed to be so far ahead of me.

Without saying a word, I followed her back into the school. And then, I went to the same place I'd been hiding all morning—the girl's bathroom—where I stayed until I stopped my angry shaking.

I hated Joshua Juaquin.

This was all his fault.

But there was no way this was going to end like science fair, with him getting the ribbon and all the attention. I was going to show him who was really in charge!

Chapter Eight
RISKY BUSINESS

Still Friday, February 4, the day that would never end

I've never been so grateful for the last bell and the weekend.

"Hey, Suki," Marley called out as I rushed down the long hall toward the front door to the school. "Don't forget, we're coming over after dinner to build the dog trap." "We" meant her and Rotem.

I tipped my head a little, but didn't stop to talk about it. I had to get out of there. Every fiber in my body was still wound up with what had happened. I was a twisted Slinky inside and the thoughts in my head were really loud. I walked toward home, talking to myself in my mind:

There's still a whole week before Valentine's Day. Ten days! I can get it done!

Then another thought countered that, saying:

We really should be much further along.

I fought that thought with:

Nuh-uh! There's plenty of time left to organize everything. Especially if I get supplies this weekend and maybe have a few people over to cut more heart cards. Shouldn't JJ have been focused on selling cards rather than arranging for people to deliver them? That's what should come first.

Yeah. That last thought quieted the opposing force in my head. I knew the right way to do the cards. JJ was way off, and Mrs. Choi, well, she'd gotten swept into his deception. He didn't care about the cards. He just wanted to beat me out as the leader.

Maybe instead of cutting hearts by myself later, I'd ask Marley and Rotem to help. They were coming over anyway. That was a start. They'd be my first official volunteers.

I was so caught up in going back and forth with my thoughts and plans that I didn't realize I was passing the park until I was through it. I didn't have to be at the shelter for half an hour, and I'd planned to spend that time in the park searching for Cinnamon Bun. I didn't have a Cinnamon Swirl drink, but I had some of the meaty dog treats from the shelter in my backpack.

Spinning on a heel, I turned back toward the bench where Marley and I first saw Cinnamon Bun. I was nearly there when I saw the golden flash by the playground. All thoughts of JJ and the Cupid Cards left my head as I dropped my backpack on the grass and took off running.

By the time I got to the swings, the dog was gone and I started to doubt if I'd seen her at all.

"Hey," a voice shouted from behind me, over by where I'd left my pack. "Get away from there, you mangy mutt!"

I raised my head to see Cinnamon Bun hovering over my backpack. She was digging at the outside pocket with her paws.

"Oh," I said out loud. She had found the treats in my bag!

I was still wearing my boots, which weren't made for running, but I took off again.

"Shoo! Shoo!" the older man who'd found the dog and my pack was yelling. "Get out of here!" He kicked my backpack.

"No!" I yelled. "Grab the dog!"

"Dogs should not be running loose in the park!" the man called out. "Who knows what diseases they might be carrying!"

I finally made it back across the park.

"Is this dog yours?" the man asked. I shook my head no as I leaned on my knees to catch my breath. My heart was racing and I was sweating. My hair was a disaster and my cheeks were flushed.

Cinnamon Bun was cute as ever, though. She glanced up at me, then stuffed her pretty little head into the outside pocket of my pack where the treats were.

I couldn't believe it. It was her! It was really her! Cinnamon Bun—just the way I remembered. Adorable. Amazing. There was a mischievous twinkle in her eye.

I managed to steady my breathing and bent down slowly.

She looked up at me. I swear she was smiling at me. Then . . .

"Shoo!"

I'd forgotten about the old man. Now that I was nearby, I could see he was about my grandpa's age, and that he carried a metal cane. He smacked the air near Cinnamon Bun with the cane. "Go! Get! Gone!" He waved the cane wildly. I could tell he thought he was protecting me.

"No!" I tried to stop him, but it was too late.

Cinnamon Bun jumped back and out of the way as the cane smacked down hard on my pack. The sound was like a slap.

"Get!" the man repeated, smacking the backpack again with the cane.

"Wait!" I shouted, then in my best command voice, "Stay! Sit! Lay down!"

The dog looked up. I could tell she wasn't afraid—more startled and confused—but still, before the cane crashed down a third time, she ran away.

I wasn't fast enough or in good enough shape to chase her again. All I could do was stare as the golden dot of *my* dog's fur popped through those thick, prickly bushes and disappeared.

"You're welcome," the old man said. He scooped up my backpack strap on the end of his cane and swung it over to me.

Tears pushed at the back of my eyes. But even in a situation like this, Mom would kill me if I wasn't polite, so I slipped my backpack off the tip of his cane and mumbled "Thanks," while putting the straps over my shoulders.

"No need to thank me. Just stay in school and don't do drugs," the man said, then headed out of the park, whistling cheerfully.

Looking back every few seconds in the direction Cinnamon Bun disappeared, I hurried away from the park toward the shelter.

I was so frustrated. Cinnamon Bun had been so close, but I couldn't rescue her. I knew Marley and Rotem would help me try again tomorrow, but I wanted her to be with me tonight. Safe and warm in my house. Curled up on my bed.

When I had said "Thanks" to the old man, I didn't mean it. No thanks to him, the best dog on the planet was back out on the street with the coyotes.

That last thought made me quicken my steps. When I got to the shelter, I burst in through the door.

"Call animal control," I announced to Mrs. Ryan, who was busy helping a man get a cat into a carrier cage. The cat was protesting wildly.

"Suki," Mrs. Ryan said in a cool voice. "I'm busy. Go to the back and ask Ben for your assignment."

"But it's an emergency," I told her, the words rushing out. "That dog. The one I want to adopt—she was in the park . . ." Over the sound of the cat's meows, I rattled on about the man, the backpack, the cane, and coyotes.

"Suki!" Mrs. Ryan put up a hand to stop me. "I don't have time for this now. I need you to let me finish here. And you need to go to the back room."

"I—" The expression on her face was a mix of frustration, anger, and disappointment. I was pretty sure the last two expressions were for me.

"Sorry," I muttered. It was probably too late for animal control to find Cinnamon Bun by the park, anyway.

In a softer and calmer tone, I asked, "Can I help get the cat ready for her new home? I could hold the cage door while you push her in."

"We've got this," Mrs. Ryan told me; a long strand of hair fell into her eyes. "You should help Ben with Bowzer."

I walked toward the back, feeling down. It was another day without Cinnamon Bun.

"Hey," Ben greeted me. He was standing by the long counter where the dog food was kept. Since I was late, Ben had already begun filling bowls with the small chunky brown pellets that smelled like grease and dirt. The big bag said CHICKEN AND RICE, but the pellets didn't look like either of those things.

"Your mom said to help with Bowzer," I told him while I took my volunteer shirt from my backpack and slipped it over the other shirt I was wearing. I didn't want to waste time changing.

Ben wasn't wearing his volunteer shirt. I wondered if it was because he was wearing a really cool '90s band shirt and refused to take that off, or that he'd just forgotten it.

"Big Bow-Wow's not eating," Ben told me. "You've met that nasty beast, right?"

"Yeah," I said, glancing at the massive lump of fur lying on the nearby cage floor. "How are you going to convince him to eat without losing your fingers?"

"No clue." Ben shrugged. "Help me put out the other dog bowls and we'll face the monster dog last." He added, "I've been considering feeding him one of the puppies. I think he'd eat that. Nutritious and delicious."

I was starting to understand Ben's sick sense of humor. I gave him a small smile instead of freaking out.

I couldn't help constantly peeking at Bowzer as Ben and I set out food in each of the shelter's cages. I refilled water bowls. The other dogs seemed so happy as they bounded toward dinner. But Bowzer didn't move.

"You sure he's alive?" I whispered to Ben, when it was the monster dog's turn to be fed.

Ben coughed and Bowzer looked up for a second, then lowered his head to the floor. He was alive, but clearly miserable.

"When did he stop eating?" I asked. I was pretty sure he'd been eating yesterday.

"Last night," Ben said, stopping in front of the big cage. Bowzer was curled up in a large furry ball. This time, he didn't bother to raise his head and look at us. I stood for a moment, watching his chest to make sure he was breathing. "Did you call a vet?" I asked, feeling concerned. He might be the meanest dog on the planet, but still, something was wrong. No dog deserved to look that sad.

Ben paused at my question and sighed.

"What?" I asked him, turning my head to face

him. Ben was a little taller than me and I had to look up. "Did you call the vet?" I repeated.

Very slowly, Ben raised one shoulder. "No."

"Why not?" I asked. Ben didn't respond.

This conversation was strange. Why was Ben being so weird and not answering?

Instead of badgering him with more questions, I decided to do what my dad would do when I wasn't answering him.

I put my hands on my hips and stared at him. And stared and stared and stared . . .

"Okay! Fine!" Ben said at last. He glanced over his shoulder at the door to the lobby, where his mom was still working.

The door was shut. We were the only volunteers around.

Ben lowered his voice to a whisper and said, "We can't afford a vet."

"But doesn't the shelter get money from the city?" I'd learned that in my orientation yesterday.

"Not enough to keep the dogs alive if they aren't adopted." Ben moved back from Bowzer's cage, as if that big dog could hear us, and dropped his voice to an even quieter whisper. "We need donations." He bobbled Bowzer's food bowl between his hands. "It's been a bad few months, so we had to stop calling the vet. It was too expensive."

"So what's going to happen?" I asked, my mind spinning. I wanted to help, but I was only a kid! "What about the vet that checks out the new strays?"

"A volunteer doctor comes once a month, but not more than that," Ben said. He looked past me to Bowzer. "The vet was already here this month for the puppies. We'd have to pay if she came back, and we can't afford it."

I got the impression that, since Bowzer couldn't ever be adopted, he was low on the priority list. Healthy puppies came first.

"But—" I started. Wouldn't a nice vet want to help poor Bowzer? He looked so pathetic.

Ben stopped me. "I'm with you, and believe me, I tried to argue," he said. "But Mom said we'll just help Bowzer as well as we can until Dr. Drew comes back or we get some more donations."

"And what if more donations don't come?" I asked, worried about the answer.

Ben was back to not talking about it. He shrugged. "My mom used to be a realtor," he said, then pinched his lips shut. I understood: without more money, the shelter would shut down forever.

Now it was my turn to sigh. These were what my mom and dad called "adult problems." What could Ben and I do? Could the shelter really close and Mrs. Ryan go back to selling houses? What would happen to the dogs? The cats? The bunny?

There was only one thing I could think of doing that could help.

I took the food bowl from Ben's hands and turned to the big dog slumped down in the big cage.

"Okay, Meanie," I said. "I'm not afraid of you. The vet won't come for you, so . . . I'm taking over. You are going to eat!" I hoped my voice sounded firm and not shaky. I had a little flashback to when he pounced on me for the treat. Bowzer had some sharp-looking teeth.

I took a step forward and held out the bowl. Like I'd done with the cinnamon bun drink in the park, I used my hand to waft the stinky scent of dog food pellets toward the furry giant.

"Bowzer, listen up. I'm going to open the cage door," I told him. "Be a good doggie. . . ."

Chapter Nine
GAME ON

That same Friday night

Well, I ended up with three stitches and a tetanus shot.

"Does it hurt?" Marley asked. I was under the covers, in pajamas, elevating my left hand on a pillow.

"Sort of," I told her. "The nurse gave me a little shot to numb the spot when the doctor did the stitches."

"That dog sounds awful," Marley said.

"It wasn't Bowzer's fault," I told her for the third time. I'd explained it to my mom and dad several times, too, when they took me to the clinic. I didn't want anyone to be mad at Bowzer. He was just being a dog.

"I brought in the bowl. Bowzer refused to eat and even scooted away. So I pushed the bowl closer. I shoved it a little too hard, and the bowl bumped his chin. Food spilled out. So I started to clean it up," I said. "Bowzer was watching my every move, but didn't come near me."

That's when everything went wrong.

I continued, "Then Mrs. Ryan came in, saw me in the cage, and freaked out. She yelled, 'Suki, what are you doing?' Bowzer didn't react, but she really startled me. I jumped backward, and the cage door accidentally slammed on my fingers."

There had been a lot of blood. Like, a horror movie amount.

Mrs. Ryan apologized for scaring me, but the truth was, I wasn't supposed to be inside Bowzer's cage. I should have slipped the food in and closed the door.

While I was gushing blood, Ben wrapped my fingers in a clean towel. He distracted me by talking about music. Ben had been taking guitar lessons for a few years. So I told him about Marley's band. It kept my mind off the pain.

"I think he was disappointed my fingers didn't get chopped off," I told Marley. We both laughed, which hurt a little because it made my hand shake.

"Since the cage door was metal, I had to get a tetanus shot," I said, tipping my elbow so my best friend could see the small Band-Aid near my shoulder.

"You're lucky that's all that happened!" Marley exclaimed. "I don't think you should go back to the shelter."

What? That was crazy-talk. I was totally going back.

I could have been fired from volunteering, but Mrs. Ryan thought I'd learned an important lesson. Mom and Dad said I'd learned something, too. I'm not sure what I learned. Maybe to not let Mrs. Ryan scare me? Or don't scratch yourself on metal? Or that shots hurt?

I was also starting to like that dumb big dog. He had rubbed his head on my leg after I got hurt, when I was still in the cage. I think he was saying, "Sorry."

"I'm going to the shelter tomorrow," I assured her. "Right after we catch Cinnamon Bun." There was an empty cage where Cinnamon could stay while I worked. I had it all planned out, and even with my bad fingers, before I left the shelter, I made sure to put down clean bedding.

"I'm heading to Rotem's to finish the trap after I leave here," Marley said.

"I don't think I can help build the trap tonight," I told her with a yawn.

My eyelids were feeling heavy. I didn't think it was the shots, but maybe. It could have just been that the day was long and pretty rotten. It was late, too. I was so, so tired. I yawned again.

"That's okay," Marley told me. "We've got it covered. I convinced Rotem that the obstacle course and the rover were too complicated."

"Good." That was a relief.

"We scaled it all down, and it's ready to roll!" she told me. "Just some treats, a cage, and peanut butter." She sighed. "I did promise he could still have a Cinnamon Bun perimeter, since that was his favorite part. And I thought you could get the coffee. Think you can meet us at the park at ten?"

"I'll be there," I said with another yawn. I assumed I'd be awake by then, but the way I felt, I thought I might sleep for days. My pillow felt so soft and my bed was more comfortable than ever. I struggled to keep my eyes open.

After that, I don't remember Marley leaving. I must have crashed.

My alarm woke me up at nine thirty the next day. Marley must have set it, because I know I didn't.

I stood and stretched, feeling good. Nothing hurt. I wiggled my fingers and then reconsidered. They did hurt a little, so that meant I'd have to make sure to hold Cinnamon Bun's leash in my right hand.

I got dressed in my favorite t-shirt and jeans with holes in both knees, then grabbed a zip-up sweatshirt and went down to breakfast.

Yesterday was a disaster, but today was a fresh start.

I briefly remembered JJ, Mrs. Choi, the volunteers . . . but then I put it all in a mental closet and closed the door.

This was going to be the best day ever. I was going to get a jump on Cupid Cards. To beat JJ, sales had to start Monday, so I needed a table, decorations, and as many hearts as I could cut. I was going to text some kids from student council to see if they could come over. Plus, Marley had already agreed to help, because that's what besties do. (I was too tired to get started last night, but I was sure she'd be on board whenever I needed her.)

And then, there was the bigger, even better, part of the day—today, Cinnamon Bun would be mine.

The sign on the coffee shop door said HAPPY SATURDAY.

"Yes, it is," I said to the sign as I pushed open the door.

JJ and Olivia were sitting at a side table with paper and pens. It looked like they were making a shopping list for the Cupid Cards. Shoot. I wasn't as ahead of them in my planning as I'd hoped.

I turned away from JJ and Olivia. They were not going to ruin my day.

"One Cinnamon Bun Swirl," I ordered. "Grande Plus." That would be enough for me and to drip around the "perimeter" to attract my new dog.

I stood to the side of the coffee bar to wait for my drink, and kept my eyes to the floor. I wanted the barista to hurry, but he wasn't getting my psychic messages and was ignoring the loud tapping of my toe.

"Hi, Suki." It was Olivia. "Whatcha doin'?"

"Nothin'," I replied.

"Oh." She paused, then said, "JJ and I have some questions about the Cupid Cards." I wasn't surprised. "And we'd like your help." Okay, that part surprised me.

"Why?" I found myself asking. I glanced past Olivia to JJ. He was holding the pen against his lips, deep in thought. I saw him write something down, then cross it out.

"As you know, JJ's determined to sell more Cards this year than last," she told me.

I held back from groaning, "Duh."

"Look, Suki, I know you liked JJ in the fourth grade, and were mad when I dated him, but isn't it time to get over that?"

"Uh, what?" That wasn't where I thought this was going.

"So maybe we can make a peace treaty and, in exchange, you can tell us ways to make everything run a lot smoother?"

"I—" Wow. What on earth? I never liked JJ. I never was jealous of them. Is that really what the two of them thought? I didn't even know where to start my argument. "No, no, no. You've got it all wrong," I said, warming up. But I wasn't sure what else to say. Though I certainly wasn't going to help them with the Cupid Cards.

I was grateful when I heard the barista call my name.

"Bye," I said, spinning around so fast my hair whipped my face. I took my cup from the barista with a fake smile, then scooted out of the shop as fast as I could walk with a hot drink and a stitched-up hand.

Thankfully, my legs were just fine.

Marley and Rotem were sitting on the park bench. I imagined hanging out there with Cinnamon Bun once she was mine. I was starting to think of the bench as our special spot.

"Yo!" I called out as I got close. I took a sip of my drink and wondered if I should have bought drinks for Marley and Rotem. Not sure how I'd have carried them, though, with only one good carrying hand.

"Yo to you," Marley replied, raising her head.

Rotem scooted away from her, snapping his book shut before I reached them. He stood. "Let's get started." It was then I notice the bag by the tree. It was a full-size wheeled duffle, like the one I took to camp every summer. The bag was so packed, it was bulging.

Rotem opened the zipper and began to bring pieces of the trap out, laying each one on the lawn as he went.

First there was a cage. I was surprised at how small it was, but Cinnamon was a small dog. The solid box tilted slightly left, but otherwise, it seemed to be pretty solid construction.

I couldn't really remember what Marley had said when she was over, other than that the plan had been scaled back. But I was happy to see that they'd ditched nearly everything in Rotem's original plan, besides the cage. This was much better. After it was set up, they put a spoonful of peanut butter inside it. The puppy would go in the cage to lick the spoon, and we'd close the door. Easy as that.

"We're set," Rotem told me. "All we need is you to dribble Swirl out and around the park, then we can set out treats to bring Cinnamon Bun close enough to smell the peanut butter."

"He's a genius, right?" Marley beamed.

"Uh, sure." I was a little distracted. I really wanted to get Marley away and alone for a second. I wanted to tell her what had happened at the coffee shop.

While Rotem scooped peanut butter into a spoon, Marley beat out a rhythm on the side of the wooden dog trap. "We're looking for a dog so sweet. Four feet and no defeat." She threw back her hair and laughed. "My new hit. I'll call it 'Ode to a Dogcatcher'!"

"There's no such thing," I told her. "It has to be an 'Animal Control Anthem.'"

"'Canine Cage Chorus,'" Marley said, getting into the groove.

"'Bow-wow Band—'" I started, when a flash of golden fur caught my eye.

Cinnamon Bun was here!

Chapter Ten
DISASTER

Saturday, February 5

"We aren't ready! Suki hasn't spilled any of the drink! Abort mission!" Rotem shouted. "New strategy!"

Of course he had a backup plan. But what was it?

I found out when, quick as a flash, Rotem grabbed a net out of the big bag. It was like one of those butterfly nets on a long stick.

"Rotem looks like an animal control . . . catcher!" I laughed.

By the look on his face, I'm pretty sure he didn't think I was funny. "Bring the dog this way," he told me in a calm voice. "Forget making a perimeter. Drip your drink to make a path, and I'll net her!"

That seemed like a practical idea. But I decided to go with my own idea.

I was pretty close to Cinnamon Bun, so I figured I should just go for it and grab her. It wasn't what the Dog-Talker, or any other expert, might say to do, but this was my show now.

I set down my cup on the ground and took off the lid.

"What are you doing?" I heard Rotem ask. "That's not the plan."

"New plan," I called out.

"No new plan," Rotem shouted to me. But I was already charting a new course of action.

Cinnamon Bun stood near the bushes, watching me cautiously. If I didn't play this right, I knew she'd be through those bushes and gone in a blink.

I sat down so I was less threatening. I jiggled the cup, and said softly, "Come on, you know you want it. Come."

She seemed to nod, and moved in closer. I poured out some drink, and she lapped it up with her cute pink tongue. A little foam settled on her nose.

Cinnamon Bun was the most adorable dog ever! Happiness swelled inside me.

"Good girl," I said. This was better than the dog treat or robot plan. She was so close—I reached forward, ready to hug her tight, when, suddenly, Rotem shouted "Gotcha!" from behind me, and leapt forward with the net, swinging it through the air.

He missed the dog. I heard him mutter, "Didn't account for wind."

Cinnamon Bun, of course, was scared by the shouting and the swinging net. She looked at me like I'd betrayed her, and made a dash toward the bushes. I knew what would happen next. It had happened twice before.

I knew what I had to do. It was bold and daring—and kind of dumb, because I forgot for a second about the stitches in my hand.

There wasn't time to go around the bushes. Cinnamon Bun went under them. So I backed up a few feet and dove over them.

I landed with a painful thud on the other side, using my hands to break my fall as I rolled onto the sidewalk. Ouch! I looked at my injured hand and could tell it was bleeding.

There was no time to think about it. I scrambled to my feet and started running after that speedy little golden blur.

"We're coming!" I heard Marley behind me.

"I have the net," Rotem put in.

"We'll go around," Marley said, as they reached the bushes.

I chased Cinnamon Bun down between two buildings. I'd forgotten how many apartments were over in this area.

The dog passed a big swimming pool and then slowed down on the other side of it. She glanced over at me, then rushed toward a short building where the first-floor apartments had small backyards. I could see patio umbrellas peeking over the top of what I imagined to be little grassy areas. Up higher, the apartments had balconies.

"Cinnamon Bun!" I called out again, realizing that actually wasn't her name. Did she even have a name? I tried "Come!" and "Sit," though those commands hadn't worked before. No name. No training. This was discouraging.

I was out of breath and tired. I didn't know how to catch her and she seemed to have endless energy.

Marley and Rotem weren't there to help yet. They probably lost me around the pool.

A quick bark brought my attention back to Cinnamon Bun—and then I saw her duck through a hole in one of those apartment yard fences and disappear from sight.

Ha! That was actually the best thing that could have happened. Cinnamon Bun had gotten herself trapped! All I had to do was block up the fence on my side, and she'd be stuck. I found a cardboard box in a nearby dumpster and hurried to cover the hole. I stuffed the box into the opening, smiling the entire time.

Next, I would knock on the door, explain that my dog was stuck in the backyard, and go get her! The leash was still in my backpack in the park, so I'd have to carry her with my cut hand, but it would be worth the pain!

I walked slowly to catch my breath while I went to the path that led around the front of the building. That's when Marley and Rotem caught up.

"Sorry the trap didn't work," Marley said. She was in way better shape than me and wasn't breathing heavy at all.

"Had you both kept to the plan, it would have worked," Rotem said between gasps. "The calculations were perfect."

"Too bad the dog doesn't do math," I replied with a chuckle.

When he fully caught his breath, he said, "That could be the project that would win me the Nobel Prize! If I can teach a dog math . . ."

Marley gave him a friendly shove. "Ridiculous!"

"Maybe I can teach the dog to count the beats in music," Rotem suggested. "It combines math and musicality. You'd like that, right?"

"Can you do that?" Marley's eyes brightened. She smiled. "But how would Cinnamon Bun hold the drumsticks?"

Even I laughed at that.

We reached the front of the apartments. I had counted the backyards and the front doors so I was certain we were at the right place.

Marley and Rotem stood behind me.

I knocked.

A tall, thin, very familiar-looking woman answered the door.

"Can I help you?" She looked at my hands as if I was

selling something. I hid my bloody fingers behind my back.

"My dog ran through a hole in your fence," I explained. "I trapped her in your yard."

"Oh?" She looked back toward a long glass door behind her. "Hang on."

I heard her shout to someone, "Sweetie, there are some kids here who say they trapped their dog in the yard. Can you look and see if there's an extra dog out back?"

There was a moment of silence, then footsteps. I saw the shadow of a boy go out the back door. I watched as he scooped up a golden furball and walked into the light.

Yes! It was Cinnamon Bun.

And—wait. The boy carrying her was Joshua Juaquin.

That was why the woman looked familiar. She was his mom. The mayor!

"The only dog in the yard was Sandy," JJ told his mom before realizing it was me at the door. "Suki?" he asked, nestling the dog—his dog—closer to his chest. He peered behind me. "Marley? Rotem? What are you guys doing here?"

Marley hadn't caught on yet, but I had. She started saying, "Suki's dog, Cinn—"

I kicked the side of her foot.

"She must have gone a different way," I said, feeling a choke in my throat. "She's lost."

"Want me to help you find her?" JJ offered. "I can go grab some shoes."

"No," I said. "Thanks." I stumbled backward. I couldn't even look at the dog in his arms. JJ's dog Sandy was Cinnamon Bun. This was a disaster.

I muttered something like, "There's a hole in your fence." And then I swept past Marley and Rotem, and, holding back my tears, rushed quickly away.

chapter eleven
TRICKY TRAINING

Rotten Saturday, February 5, the worst day ever

When I got home, I shut the front door so quietly, it made my mom come running. Seriously, that woman has the best hearing.

I had one foot on the steps to go up to my room when she touched my arm.

"Suki? What's going on?" Mom asked, taking a long look at my face. She was still in her teaching clothes—bra top and stretchy shorts. It would have been embarrassing if we were in public. I was secretly proud of my mom's passion, but I'd never tell her that.

I felt so weak and messy. If I had to answer, I knew I'd start crying again.

"Come on." She led me upstairs and tucked me into bed. With gentle footsteps, she left the room. Then with the same quiet steps, she came back carrying a cup of hot tea.

I sat up and took the steaming mug. For a long moment, I just stared into it. How could this have happened? Not only was Cinnamon Bun not a stray, she belonged to—of all people—JJ! *Argh!* She'd been JJ's dog all along. His yard just had a hole in the fence. I couldn't believe it.

I remembered JJ talking about getting a dog from the shelter the day that we met Cinnamon Bun. Which meant that she actually might have been a stray at some point before he picked her out. But then she got adopted by JJ, my sworn enemy! Couldn't I have found her earlier?

Not that I would've been allowed to keep her.

I thought I'd had other worst days before, but this one was the new worst.

JJ had won the science fair. He was Mrs. Choi's favorite for Cupid Cards. And now he stole my dog!

I pushed the teacup into my mom's hand and

flopped back into my pillows. I felt like a building had crashed on top of me. It hurt that much.

Mom said softly, "We can talk when you're ready." She got up again and went into the bathroom. Bringing back a wet washcloth, Mom cleaned off my bloody stitches and re-bandaged my hand.

I breathed heavily. It would help to talk about it.

"Mom," I said at last. "There's this boy at school."

Her eyebrows raised.

I went on. "Not like that. He . . ." I blurted out the only thing I could think of. "I hate him." Then went on. "And there's this dog." Slowly, I told her the whole story, from the Cupid Cards to finding Cinnamon Bun in the park to chasing her back to JJ's house.

I expected her to say, "You couldn't have had a dog anyway, Suki." Instead, Mom said, "Some things happen for a reason."

That was frustrating. I said angrily, "This happened for *no* good reason. *Nothing* positive will come out of it." I wiped away a small tear that leaked out of my eye. "Everything is ruined *forever*."

Mom handed me a tissue off the nightstand and stood. "Forever is a long time. Open your heart, Suki. You'll see . . ."

Ugh. So cheesy. Then Mom kissed me on the forehead and told me when dinner would be ready. I spent the rest of the afternoon watching videos about dogs online and organizing the stuff I'd bought for the Cupid Cards. I even made some nice decorations for my own sale table. And I did some homework. By the time I went to sleep, I was exhausted.

Sunday morning, I wouldn't have gotten out of bed if I hadn't agreed to work at the shelter again. I was already late from pressing SNOOZE a million times. I got dressed quickly, changed the bandage on my hand, and grabbed a granola bar on my way out.

The sunlight felt blinding.

"Suki!" Ben called my name from Marley's garage. What was he doing there?

I was already late to the shelter, so I figured another couple minutes wouldn't matter. Plus, I'd just tell Mrs. Ryan I was with her son. Parents usually forgive stuff like that.

I walked slowly over to Marley's driveway. I wanted to move faster, I really did. I was just feeling so completely *blah*.

"Hey," he said, setting down a guitar and coming

out to meet me. "Thanks for telling me about the band. Marley said I could join."

"Cool," I said, without emotion.

Marley and Rotem were warming up. She was on drums and he was playing keyboard. I knew Rotem played bass guitar, so keys was probably new. But knowing him, he'd likely learn the clarinet, ukulele, a harmonica, and the tuba next. He'd be great at all of it.

Marley rushed over, pushed past Ben, and gave me a hug. "Sorry about Cinnamon Bun."

"Yeah," Rotem said, not raising his head from the keys.

I realized I'd left them to clean up the mess from the dog trap. I apologized to them for that, too. They'd worked really hard on it.

"That's okay," Rotem told me. "We can use the parts for something else."

"Like what?" I wondered.

He shrugged. "When I know, I'll tell you."

"Isn't he clever?" Marley said, looking at him with a grin. Suddenly, I realized that maybe there was something up between them. I'd missed the signs: the close talking, the endless planning . . . and Marley's newly sparkling eyes. Now it seemed so obvious!

I was so absorbed in my own problems, I hadn't seen that Marley liked Rotem! I also think he liked her, but I wondered if he realized it. I was happy for them. I could now see them as a really cute couple. I wondered when it would become official and if they'd mind having me drag along as a third wheel. Would they do anything special for Valentine's Day?

"Suki." Ben dragged back my attention. "When you see my mom, can you do me a fave?"

"Sure," I said, adding, "as long as it's not gross or scary."

"You're a wimp," he said. I noticed his t-shirt. It said *Bloody Heart*, and showed what looked like a heart that was ripped in two and dripping blood. I assumed Bloody Heart was a band, but the shirt was super creepy.

He caught me looking. "Bloody Heart is one of my favorite bands. I wish *this* band had a name that was anywhere near as awesome," he told me. "I know this is only my first practice, but I'm already dreading telling people I'm in the Happy Little Llamas. It's horrible! How are we going to get any rock-respect with that name?"

I shrugged, not sure what to say. Luckily, Ben went back to asking the favor. "Don't tell my mom I told you about the money problems at the shelter. I think she'd be mad if she knew I told you." He leaned in and lowered his voice. "I only know because I was there when the mayor came to get a dog the other day, and I overheard them talking."

"The mayor?" Ah, crud-potatoes. That must have been when she went to get Cinnamon Bun. The thought felt like a sharp pain.

"She needed photos of her doing something nice for the community, so she brought a camera crew when she came to adopt a dog for JJ," Ben said. "I heard my mom tell her about the money problem, and the mayor said she didn't have the budget to help, still, they'd try to figure out something."

"I'm sure she will," I said sarcastically. I wouldn't depend on JJ's mom to solve this!

"Just don't tell Mom, okay?" Ben said. I agreed, and an instant later, Marley called him for practice.

"Ben! No more yapping!" She smiled at me. "No offense, Suki, but I need him now."

I laughed. "I'm late anyway. Adios!"

As I walked away, I heard Ben try to sway Marley on the band name. "How about a compromise?" Ben said. "We could be the Bloody Little Llamas."

I didn't have to hear Marley's response. I knew exactly what she'd say.

When I opened the door to the animal shelter, Mrs. Ryan wasn't mad that I was late. She did want me to hurry, though.

"Suki, I need you to go to the puppy class." She pointed the way through a side door into the open classroom area. "The regular assistant is home with the flu. Ask Alexandra what to do." Alexandra was the teacher. We'd met once before.

The puppy class was twice a week. Once on Wednesday evening, the time I'd first come into the shelter, and a second time on Sunday mornings.

I'd forgotten that Olivia and Luna were in the class until I opened the door.

"Hi," Olivia greeted me. Did she already forget what she'd said at the coffee shop? The thing about me being jealous when she dated JJ? I couldn't believe she thought that. *Ew.*

Luna began pulling on the leash, trying to get to me. I walked over and squatted down. My feelings toward Olivia weren't Luna's fault.

"Hey, Lu," I said, petting the dog's warm head.

Luna pounced forward and licked my face. She was all over me as she stood on her hind legs and bounced.

Olivia pulled back on the leash. "Ouch!" she exclaimed as she held the leash tight. It was then I noticed that Olivia's fingers were red and rough. They looked blistered.

"Back. Down. Luna, No." Olivia tried every command, as she shifted the leash in her hand to make it hurt less.

"It's all right," I said, pushing Luna off me and standing up. "I'll find out what we are doing today. I think she'll be an easier dog if you can teach her to sit and stay." She also needed to learn not to jump on people.

Walking away, I felt okay about how I behaved with Olivia. I wasn't friendly, but I wasn't *not* friendly, either.

The instructor, Alexandra, was young, a little round, and had the nicest smile.

"We are going to work on 'Come' and 'Sit' commands today," Alexandra told me, while stuffing her pockets with little chewy treats. "And we should review crate training for puppies, because I'm sure that there are a few people who let the dogs sleep on their beds." She shook her head. "It's a big no-no."

I had spent a lot of time learning about dogs, but working with them in reality was hard. I listened to Alexandra's lesson and then helped with everything she asked me to. She was working a lot with Luna, and I helped a German shepherd puppy sit by pushing down his tushy when his owner, an older woman, gave the command. I also helped a super adorable bulldog puppy, who had such a fat little body. When he sat, it looked like he had no legs. I couldn't always tell if he was sitting or lying down.

Near the end of class, Alexandra explained crate training.

"Giving your puppy his own personal bedroom will make him feel secure," she said. "And it's the best way to potty-train. When the dog isn't with you, he's in the crate." She talked while I handed out brochures. "There's no playtime without going outside first. And when you can't supervise the dog, he or she always goes back in the crate." I'd never crate trained a dog myself, but by the time Alexandra was done talking, I felt like I could. Maybe I could've tried to if I'd gotten Cinnamon Bun instead of dumb JJ. I bet he was even letting her sleep in his bed.

When the class ended, Alexandra told me, "You did great today!"

Pride swept over me. It pushed back some of my harder feelings.

I was even happier when Alexandra asked, "Can you come to all the classes to help out?"

Did I answer? I think I did, but maybe I just whooped and jumped around a bit.

Olivia was still there, getting Luna's things together for the walk home. I was in such a good mood, I went up to her and asked, "How's it going?"

"Luna did okay," Olivia said. But then, Luna jumped up on me. "She needs more classes." Olivia shrugged and pulled her down, then said, firmly, "Luna, sit!" Luna just stared up at her, not sitting. I slipped Olivia one of the treats I had in my pocket and she tried again. This time, Luna sat!

"Thanks, Suki," she said, beaming at her dog.

I rubbed Luna's head. "You're a good dog," I cooed. Luna happily pushed her head into my hand, begging to be scratched more.

I walked with Olivia and Luna to the shelter door even though I wasn't leaving yet. I had work to do, feeding the dogs and cleaning up poop. Plus, I wanted to visit Bowzer and see how he was doing.

"Can I tell you something?" Olivia said as we stood at the main door.

"Sure," I said. Through the glass, I noticed JJ outside on the sidewalk. He must have come to walk her home. He didn't have Cinn—I mean, Sandy—with him.

She glanced at JJ and waved, but didn't open the door to the shelter.

"The cards stuff is not going very well," she admitted. "We cut a bunch of red paper hearts yesterday." Olivia held up her rough and red fingers. I didn't tell her that I'd already noticed how bad they were.

"Cutting those hearts was a lot of work." She sighed. "JJ's my best friend, but I don't know if this is going to work. He wants to sell more cards than ever, but we didn't make even close to a thousand. And even though we worked really late last night, we ran out of time to tape the candy on them. How are we going to sell cards if we can't make them?"

Wow. Never expected that. Not in a million years. I held back a smug smile.

"What are you going to do?" I asked, curious. I reminded myself silently that this was what JJ did to me. He took my ideas. So why not dig a little and see what I could get in return?

"I don't know . . ." Olivia replied, her voice a little sad. "But sales start tomorrow."

My sales were starting tomorrow, too, but unlike Olivia and JJ, I was prepared. I mean, I also didn't have a thousand cut cards, but I wasn't going to need that many on the first day.

Marley and Rotem had said they'd come help me cut the cards today, but both canceled at the last minute. To make up for it, Marley said she'd make me a box for the cards to go in. I'd also texted everyone from student council to help, but everyone had an excuse. I hoped no one was at JJ's, because that would be so wrong! So it looked like I had to do it myself, even if it meant staying up late.

I set myself up for success by using my really good scissors to protect my fingers, and by taking stretching breaks. My left hand felt better, too, and that gave me confidence.

To pass the time while I cut hearts, I started watching the Dog-Talker training videos as I worked, even though I'd already seen them over and over. Doug, a.k.a. the Dog-Talker, was tall and built like a body-builder. He talked in short, direct clips with military-like commands.

Since I'd now had some real contact with dogs, I understood the lessons differently. I liked how Doug was clearly in control, but I could also see something else this time through: those dogs in the videos were definitely trained already! I couldn't believe I didn't know that before. They should have had a disclaimer at the beginning, like, "You can try this, but don't expect it to work right away. These dogs have been professionally trained. So . . . good luck!"

I was feeling annoyed when the second video came on. This was on crate training, and again, the dogs did it so easily. Now, even though I hadn't tried it myself on a real dog, I knew that was not the way it worked. Training dogs was hard. And it took time and energy. You couldn't do it in a twenty-minute video.

With new perspective, I watched the rest of Seasons 1-2 while my fingers moved pretty much on their own. By the time I was done with the videos, I had hundreds of hearts and some really good ideas of things I could try with Bowzer. I wasn't ready to give up on him like everyone else seemed to be. He was already trained like the dogs in the video, but he'd just forgotten how to behave. Thanks to the Dog-Talker, I was excited to try a new approach.

I slept really well and woke up ready for an awesome day.

Chapter Twelve
CRAZY COMPETITION

Monday, February 7

I got to school early to put my plan into action.

But JJ beat me there. He was sitting outside school trying to sell his version of Cupid Cards. *Trying*, meaning there was no line and no buyers. I wondered if any of the volunteers he'd gotten at lunch on Friday had gone to his house yesterday to help cut out hearts. I guessed not.

"Get your Cupid Cards!" JJ called out to anyone passing by. "One dollar. We'll deliver them to your friends and teachers on Valentine's Day."

I'll admit the table decoration was really cute.

There was a red tablecloth, hand-painted with pink hearts. He had a few examples of the hearts set out on the table, and a box marked PRIVATE to put them into with a slit in the top and a big padlock, as if no one would see the message you wrote to whoever you bought one for. The reality was that whoever was delivering them could see the message on the heart— it wasn't like they were in an envelope or anything.

Last year, we never told people the cards would be private. If you wanted them to be kept a secret, the deal was, don't sign your name.

I didn't walk all the way to the table, but got close enough to look. I couldn't help myself.

"Suki!" JJ shouted. "Buy some cards for your friends!"

"Negative."

"How about one for a secret crush?" He said that way too loudly. I blushed even though I didn't have a crush, secret or not.

I refused again and prepared to walk away. That was when I really noticed the paper hearts that were laying on the table.

"Huh?" I walked over and picked one up. It was not actually heart-shaped. More like a circle with a slit on top. "Are you selling Cupid Planets?" I joked. "Cupid Blobs?"

JJ frowned. He grabbed a better-looking one from a box under the table and snatched the one I was holding. "There were some scissor issues."

"Kid scissors?" I asked, though I already knew from seeing Olivia's hands that that was his problem. "You needed sharp adult ones."

"Yeah." He looked down at the heart. "I mean, these kind of look like real hearts. The ones in people's chests." It was a sad joke.

"Where's the candy?" I asked.

"Sandy ate it," he said as if that was normal. "I'm going back to the store tonight."

I hoped Sandy was okay. Dogs shouldn't eat people food, especially not a bunch of candy.

"Too bad," I said. "Now, watch and learn how it's done." Behind me, Marley and Rotem had arrived and were setting up my table. JJ was on one side of the steps leading up to the school, and I would be on the other.

My table wasn't as cutely decorated as JJ's, but my hearts were beautiful. And I actually had candy.

Once it was all set up, Marley and Rotem had to go.

I wasn't sure where JJ's team, a.k.a. Olivia, was, but right now, it was just me versus him. May the best salesperson win.

I shouted to the nearest group of kids being dropped off, "Get your *authentic* Cupid Cards here. Perfect hearts *and* candy!"

JJ went for the same sale. "Cupid Blobs here. Don't be traditional this year. Show your friends you stand out from the pack!"

"Blobs?" I yelled across the broad cement steps. "Stealing my idea again?"

He shrugged. "Not like you had a trademark on it!"

My shoulders got all tight. I had to sell more. I had to show him hearts were better than blobs. That I was better than him.

The next kid who walked by was a girl I knew. Her mom was also Japanese and we'd met at a cultural event.

"Annie!" I waved a perfect heart toward her. "Send your favorite teacher a heart to show you love class."

"Oh, good idea!" she said. Yay! She bought them for all her teachers. She wrote her messages. She picked out her lollipops, and I taped them on and took her money.

"Thanks," I said while I gently set her hearts into the designated box Marley had made for me. She had turned the dog-catching cage that Rotem had made onto its side, and covered it with cute heart-covered fabric.

When Annie walked away, I was feeling good. Then I noticed JJ had a small group around his table.

"Hmmm," I muttered. "What is he up to?" I stood up, but couldn't hear what he was telling the growing crowd around him.

Instead of trying to stop the next group of students entering school, I marched over to JJ's table and elbowed my way through about ten students, my hands on my hips. "Are you promising that no one has to go to school ever again if they buy blobs from you, or something?"

"No," he said, proudly handing me a small slip of paper.

I looked down. It was a free pizza coupon.

"Buy five blobs and get a pizza for free," JJ announced.

"Where did you get these?" I waved the coupon in his face.

"They're from the move-in packets that the city gives to new residents," JJ told me, while selling a handful of weird-looking cards to an eighth grader. "Occasionally, it pays to have your mom as the mayor." He smiled. "I know where the key to the cabinet is."

I couldn't believe it! The best I could do was some passes to a yoga class, if my mom would even go for that. Which I doubted.

"Ugh!" I exclaimed, racing back to my own table, where three girls were looking at my cards.

"These are so pretty," one of the girls gushed. "But what do we get if we buy them from you?" She glanced over her shoulder at JJ.

"Uh." I considered that. "Nice-looking hearts, with a lollipop, delivered on time to your friends?"

She tossed down the card on the table. "The ugly ones come with pizza," she declared and dragged her friends away.

When the bell rang for class, I knew that I'd sold a fraction of what JJ had managed to sell.

I was going to have to up my game.

I got the student council on my side. Well, some of them. I ran around grabbing anyone that I could find, and at the beginning of the next class period, I asked them to make an announcement about Cupid

Cards sales. By lunch, I had a good line at my table and brought in some great cash.

JJ didn't have a table in the lunchroom. Marley heard from someone (who heard from Olivia) that JJ didn't think lunch sales were important, and that he was gearing up for getting students as they left school.

Ha! That was a mistake.

I caught his eye across the lunchroom and could see he realized his error.

That was when my phone buzzed. There were no phones allowed at school except at lunch. Everyone in the entire lunchroom looked at their phone at the same time. We'd all gotten the text.

It read:

Buddy Blobs for sale after school. Not just lollipops. We have chocolate!

He'd changed the name to go with what he had! That was annoyingly smart. Also, how did he text the whole school at once? And how had he managed to get chocolate candies to school between this morning and now?

There was a second text an instant later:

Allergies? No problem. Come find JJ.

If Marley hadn't been by my side at that moment,

I'd have tossed my phone across the lunchroom at JJ's head. I had to admit, he was right to have an option for kids with allergies, though. I was just starting to speculate what that might be when a sparkling bouncy ball rolled by my feet. I picked it up.

JJ waved at me from near the trash cans.

I stuck out my tongue at him.

"Remember that whole immature baby thing?" Marley told me. "You're heading there fast."

I stuck out my tongue at her *and* blew a raspberry.

"He thinks he's so clever." I groaned. Teachers were going to hate it when little balls were bouncing all over the classrooms. But still, it was a good alternative to candy. I wished I'd thought of it.

I had to admit, JJ was pretty good at this Cupid Cards stuff. It didn't make me like him, and I'd never tell him that, but still . . .

The lunch bell rang and I still had a pretty good-sized box of hearts to sell, but I was determined to sell them all, and more. Maybe I could get Marley and the band to come help me make more tonight. Mom and Dad could cut hearts, too.

We had student council after school, but I'd already told Mrs. Choi I'd be late because of the sales. She suggested that the entire council could come outside and help us, meaning me and JJ.

It was clear that Mrs. Choi still didn't know JJ and I were having competitive blob/card sales, and I didn't think she'd be happy when she found out. So it was even more important that I showed her what I could do and get the entire council to be on my side. I had to do more to sell more!

Before class started after lunch, I was standing by my locker trying to think of ideas. I didn't have chocolates. Or a new name for the cards. Or pizza.

Hmmm . . . My head hurt from thinking.

Chapter Thirteen
A FRESH IDEA

After school, the same day

As it turned out, there was only one Cupid Cards table outside after school. It was mine. All the student council members who were there to help were helping me. I kept looking over at the spot where JJ was supposed to be with his Buddy Blobs. Where was he?

His texts had worked, and brought kids outside to the table. When everyone saw he wasn't there, they bought the cards I had instead. I sold out what I'd made. I was really excited to share my good news with Mrs. Choi.

Still, there was this small part of me that wondered: What happened to JJ?

On my way to find Mrs. Choi, I stopped to put the cards we'd sold into my locker.

While I was there, the weirdest thing happened.

A red piece of paper fluttered out of my locker and onto the floor. It was a Buddy Blob. The note side landed up and was easy to read. In thick block letters it said:

Will You Be My Valentine?

The card wasn't signed.

I bent down to pick it up just as Marley walked up. "You weren't at the meeting so I thought maybe you needed help cleaning . . ." she said. Then she saw the blob in my hands. "What's that?"

I shook my head to clear it. "I have no idea." With a shrug, I showed it to her.

"Well, well, well," she said with a laugh. "It's not even Valentine's Day yet, and Suki got a Valentine." She sang out, "Suki has a secret admirer."

"I'm sure it's nothing," I said, trying to shut her down. "Probably just a joke, or someone got the wrong locker, or something."

"I don't think so," she said in a singsong voice. "I bet it's from JJ."

"You're insane!" I said, blushing. There was no way it was from him. And even if it was, why not just deliver it with the other blobs on Valentine's Day?

Marley chuckled. "I'll bet you ten dollars he's your secret admirer."

"You're on," I said. That was the easiest ten dollars I'd ever make.

I put the card in my locker with the ones I'd sold and followed her down the hall to the meeting room.

Before we got to the classroom, Marley put out a hand to stop me. "I almost forgot," she said. "Did you hear what happened?"

"No," I said.

"JJ got busted," Marley told me.

"What?"

"Those pizza coupons he was handing out—" she started.

"Yeah?"

"They were only supposed to be for new city residents, not for hungry students!"

"What?" I started laughing. JJ wasn't so clever after all! "Where is he?" I asked as I peeked through the little window into the room where the student council meeting was held. "Is he here?" A knot was forming in my belly. Sure, I sold a lot of cards, but . . . this didn't feel so good. It was competitive, but still, I didn't want him to get in trouble over it.

Marley said, "Last period, Mrs. Choi pulled him out of class for a 'talk.' I'm guessing it was brutal."

That explained why he wasn't selling blobs at the end of the day.

JJ was sitting in the corner of the room. He was acting like everything was fine, but there was a shadow over him.

It just got worse when Mrs. Choi announced, "JJ will no longer be on the Cupid Cards project." She looked to me. "Suki will be in charge from here on out."

JJ didn't say a word.

I'd won! The Cupid Cards were mine. This was bigger than winning science fair, or any of the other times we'd competed. I'd gotten exactly what I wanted. I hadn't even had to try that hard to get rid of him.

So why didn't I feel better about it?

My head was spinning. JJ was the one who took the coupons and bribed students to buy blobs. He was the one who blew it. He'd brought trouble on himself.

And as the meeting went on, the knot in my belly grew tighter.

Mrs. Choi praised me for the sales. She was proud, just like I'd predicted.

I glanced over my shoulder at JJ while she went on to talk about the dance. They needed someone to take the lead on that part of the program. JJ was sitting on his hands. Maybe she'd told him he should never volunteer again? Would she kick him off council?

This wasn't how I wanted to succeed. This wasn't what I wanted at all. It was a dumb Valentine's Day project, not brain surgery. It wasn't like we were trying to save something important . . . like the environment, or a sick kid, or the animal shelter . . .

Oh.

Wait.

Oh . . . Oh . . . Oh!

I had a great idea—it would do more good than anything I'd ever done. But I had to put everything that had happened with JJ for the past three years aside, and focus on a *bigger* goal. If this succeeded, though, it would definitely be worth it.

"Mrs. Choi." I took a deep breath and raised my hand. "I have a great idea about Cupid Cards."

She looked at me with her head tilted. "We've moved on from Cupid Cards," she told me.

"It's important," I said, looking serious.

"Okay, let's hear it," Mrs. Choi said.

"I've changed my mind." I could not believe I was about to say this out loud. "We need to sell way more Cupid Cards than last year. There is no such thing as too many." It was hard for me to say JJ was right about anything, but I wasn't going to stop. This was too important.

Mrs. Choi looked like she was about to say something, but I hurried on with my thought. "But not for the school dance! Or not *just* for the dance. I hereby propose that we raise the minimum we need for the dance, and then anything on top of that goes to the animal shelter. I know they could use the money— and they're the only no-kill shelter in the area."

"That's a great idea!" Marley said. Mrs. Choi was smiling and agreeing, and as I looked around the room everyone was nodding their heads in agreement. Only JJ was frowning, and looking down at his lap.

But I wasn't done yet. "In order to raise more money than last year . . . I need JJ to be back on the project again," I said. Yeah, that was a big chance I was taking.

Marley was gaping at me, and JJ looked confused. I ran over to where JJ was sitting.

"Look, JJ, this competition thing isn't working," I said. "I'm just not feeling the same kind of joy as the last time I beat you." I was only half-joking.

Mrs. Choi looked at us both, confused, but I didn't think I needed to explain the whole situation at this point.

"I *let* you beat me," he said snarkily.

I rolled my eyes. But it was time to make peace— it was the only way for this to work. "Don't make me change my mind here, buddy," I said. "I thought I could do Cupid Cards alone, but actually, you were the one to motivate me to even do as much as I have now." I realized it was true as I said it. It was only the competition that had made me work so hard on the cards. "I need your help to sell as many cards as possible. I have to admit, you've had some good ideas— like texting everyone—even if not *all* your ideas were so great."

He gave me a piercing look. Maybe better never to mention the pizza coupons again.

"Truce," I said, putting out a hand.

He stared long and hard at my palm.

"Shake it, you dope," Marley said, standing up. "This grudge between you two has gone on long enough."

After a long beat, JJ reached out and reluctantly shook my hand.

I could see our teacher watching us with interest. Once again, she was letting the action play out, ready to step in if necessary.

"Let's start over," I told JJ. "Together."

JJ nodded firmly and smiled. "Let's help those animals!"

I looked at Mrs. Choi and asked, "Can we be partners again?"

At first I thought she was going to give us both a lecture, since it was probably becoming clear to her that we weren't exactly working together before. But after a second of silence, her frown faded and she nodded. "Yes. I'm proud of you, Suki," she said. "This is real leadership."

I beamed. It felt so motivated. And it felt good to not be mad at JJ!

The meeting continued, and at the end I went over to JJ again.

"We can offer a choice," I said. "Blobs or hearts. Everyone can choose what they want."

"We're going to have to make more of both," he said, standing up from his desk and meeting me eye-to-eye.

"We will!" I said.

I would gladly make a million blobs if that's what I had to do to save the shelter.

Chapter Fourteen
STICKING WITH IT

Tuesday, February 8

"We've sold a combined total of about a hundred cards today," JJ reported when I met him after the final bell. We were going to work at a table outside school, trying to get a few more sales before kids went home—and trying not to freeze. "I'll admit that I'm not sure how we are going to get to a thousand before Valentine's Day."

I had to agree. I was wearing my shelter volunteer shirt and jeans, and had made a sign about the shelter. I hoped that if we advertised we were raising money for the shelter, more kids would buy more cards.

There were blobs for sale on one side of the table and hearts on the other. Even though it wasn't really a competition anymore, it sort of was. Of the hundred cards we'd sold that day, it was pretty evenly split, but I planned to text JJ later that I beat his sales. (Though even if I didn't, that was still my plan! I wasn't even really planning to count, just text. It would be funny.)

"Hey," Olivia said, coming to stand behind the table and help.

It wasn't like I invited her or anything; she just showed up and jumped in. Maybe JJ invited her? Maybe it was Marley? Someone must have told her where we'd all be, because here she was, ready to volunteer.

"I—" I didn't know what to say. But now that I had a truce with JJ, I felt like I should try to make things better with Olivia, too.

Just then, Marley leapt over me and hugged Olivia, saying, "I'm glad you're here!" She seemed to be acting as if we were always friends with Olivia, and just hadn't seen her in a while. Olivia looked surprised, but hugged Marley back and smiled. Maybe just acting nice would be like a big magic eraser that cleaned everything up.

It felt like a good idea to follow Marley's lead. I simply decided to stop being so mad at Olivia, and to remember the days when we were friends instead. I was still far more cautious about it than Marley seemed to be, but once I let myself be okay with the idea of making up, it wasn't so hard.

Olivia was like Marley. Three seconds into it, she acted like everything was rah-rah awesome. Maybe she was ready to be friends again, too.

"Maybe we need different candy?" Olivia suggested.

"Or we could offer free donuts? I think Mom has some coupons . . ." JJ said. I looked at him to make sure he was joking, and then we all laughed.

"No free food," I said, shaking my head.

"I should have listened to you from the start," JJ admitted. "Now I realize how hard this project is." He shrugged. "I guess I kind of thought that it all just fell magically together last year."

"Right." I choked on a laugh. "Magic."

It was good to know we were on the same team at last. JJ was a lot nicer when he wasn't trying to win. I guess I was, too.

Just then, Rotem came by.

"There's something I need to ask you both," I said to him and Marley, now that they were here together.

"Is it about finding out who sent the Buddy Blob to you?" She raised a hand as if she had a magnifying glass in it. "I'm a great detective."

JJ and Rotem gave each other questioning looks.

I ignored that comment. "So I had an idea . . ." I paused. "Actually, hold on." I pulled JJ aside. If we were going to work together now, I needed to talk to him about my plan first.

So I told JJ my idea.

He was into it!

We went back to Marley and Rotem and JJ explained what we were thinking.

"On it," Marley said. She and Rotem immediately left to plan.

The wheels were in motion.

Olivia had to get home, too, so she left and JJ and I stayed and cleaned up. Then we went to talk to Principal Hollis. We had a few things to arrange to make our plan work by Friday.

I was amazed at how well we were working together. If everything went like we imagined, we'd sell way more Cupid Cards and earn a ton of money for the shelter.

Later, when I reached the animal shelter, I was feeling great. My homework was even done, and I had time to relax.

Mrs. Ryan greeted me. "What are you doing here, Suki? I feel like you're always here," she teased. "When I gave you the job, I didn't expect you to volunteer every day."

I smiled. "I want to be here!" I said. I liked school fine, but if I had to choose . . . I'd be at the shelter all day, every day, if I could.

"Of course, you're welcome anytime," she assured me. I stared toward the back when she said, "Oh, someone adopted the bunny this morning."

Okay, that made me a little sad, but happy, too. I was conflicted about the bunny. I liked him and had started bringing my leftover lunch carrots to the shelter for him. But a bunny wouldn't be my choice for a pet. I wanted a pet that could fetch and sit and catch a ball. A dog, obviously.

I decided to take my good mood and share it with the biggest grump I knew.

"Hello, Bowzer," I said quietly, approaching the monster's cage. "Today, we are becoming friends, whether you want to be friends or not. I will get you adopted, if it's the last thing I do here!"

Instead of slipping a treat through the slot in the door, or dropping his food bowl and running away, I opened the door all the way. Bowzer was doing his "I'm so depressed" face at me and didn't rise from the floor, where he looked more like a carpet than a dog.

After watching all those Dog-Talker videos, I'd read more about dogs like Bowzer online. I knew he was sad. He'd been at the shelter too long and had forgotten what it was like to be in a home. This dog needed a lot of love to teach him to trust again.

Working with a puppy like Cinnam—er, Sandy— was fun for me, but I could see that giving Bowzer new confidence was important, too. Then he could get out of the shelter and into a house where someone needed him. I wanted to help Bowzer find his forever family.

I'd read online that talking loud to a dog like him was a mistake, so I decided not to talk at all. I stepped inside, closed the door behind me, and sat down calmly on the floor.

He glanced up, but didn't move.

An hour later, Mrs. Ryan came into the back of the shelter. She started to ask what I was doing—but then she noticed that Bowzer's head was resting comfortably on my lap. His fur was surprisingly soft. He'd eaten all his food and I was petting him while he napped.

She was surprised.

I said, "Did Ben tell you that our school is raising money for the shelter?"

"Yes," Mrs. Ryan said, still staring at me with Bowzer on my lap. She rubbed her eyes as if it weren't possible. "It's very nice of you, and I really appreciate it! Look, Suki, I know you're trying so hard with everything, but I don't want you to be disappointed if things don't turn out."

I looked down at the fluff muffin now snoring and drooling on my pants. "I know," I said. She was talking about both the shelter and the dog. I sighed. "But we have to try."

Mrs. Ryan gave me a small smile. "Well, you certainly have proven you're persistent."

That I was . . . and I wasn't going to give up.

Chapter Fifteen
CUPID CRUSH

Wednesday, February 9 to Friday, February 11

Mass text messages from JJ started dinging at dinnertime.

The first one said:

Don't forget to bring $$ to buy Candy Cards tomorrow.

Even though we were selling both Buddy Blobs and heart-shaped Cupid Cards, JJ had come up with the name "Candy Cards" for all of them, which was a great name (and easier to text).

The next text popped up in the morning when I was eating breakfast. It read:

Cards4sale: Do you have ur $?

Between me, Marley, Rotem, Olivia, and JJ, we also had Candy Cards reminders on every social media site. Now that there was a real mission involved, so many people were helping pitch in!

Wednesday, we sold 300 cards.

Thursday more texts went out, and we sold 250 more. That brought us to about 850 cards sold.

I was sure we were going to hit 1,000 by Friday!

JJ was going away for the weekend with his mom, but Olivia and I talked about getting together while he was gone and cutting as many extra as the two of us could. The more we sold, the more money we'd raise for the shelter! It was all about raising as much money as possible for them. I was focused.

And our secret plan was going to take place at lunch on Friday. I was sure it would take our sales like a rocket ship to Mars. Straight to the sky!

Friday, there was magic in the air. I could feel it as I entered school. Seriously, like real magic, the kind in books and TV.

We'd already sold 1,000 cards and were heading to 1,500. That meant that kids were buying more than we ever expected. Flipping amazing!

The text reminders worked. There was a total Candy Cards craze at school. Even teachers were getting into it.

For me . . . everything was going really well, at school and at the shelter.

It had been three days since I'd first gotten into the cage with Bowzer, and I'd gone in every day since. After school today, I had permission from Mrs. Ryan to take him for our first walk!

I was floating on clouds.

Nothing could bring me down.

"Suki . . . helloooo . . . Suki . . ."

I blinked.

"It's time to start."

I blinked again. This time I noticed the group standing around me: Marley, Ben, and Rotem.

"Oh right." I stood. "Let's go!"

"We are Happy Little Llamas!" Ben was at the microphone in the center of the lunchroom. I could hear a slight moan in his voice, revealing that he was still unhappy with the name.

"And today, we rock—for the animal shelter." He pointed to the sales table in the corner. "Buy five Valentine's Day cards and get a picture with the band."

Marley thought that last bit was ridiculous, but it wasn't like we could afford t-shirts to give away or anything cool like that. Pictures with the band were free! JJ and I agreed that this was better than free pizza. Plus, no one would get in trouble.

We'd been sending out teasers and snippets of the band's music since Tuesday. It was my goal to make the Happy Little Llamas into rock stars by the time of the concert. It was funny how people got super into it.

The text we'd sent out the night before said:

Pic with HLL! Save a dog! Or cat!

(HLL was now short for Happy Little Llamas.)

I had an idea to also include a special original song to download for the biggest spender.

Ben would write it. The band would play it. Rotem would upload it. And Marley would design the cover art.

That came in a text this morning:

Biggest spender gets a fresh song download.

We had to limit the download contest just to people who bought cards today, since so many students had already bought them.

The lunch line moved fast in the back of the room as students got their trays and found seats where they could see.

The band started with a bunch of cover songs. Kids were rocking. They were eating. Dancing. And they were shopping for Cupid Cards, too.

I was selling the hearts, and JJ was selling the blobs. JJ started to high-five me after every ten cards we sold. Sales were moving so fast, half the time he'd go to high-five me, and I'd be busy selling cards myself, so he'd just give me a little smack on the back. We both laughed.

"Trade places with me," I told JJ after a while.

"What? Why?" he asked.

"Just come on, do it," I said. We swapped seats and I began to sell his blobs instead of my hearts.

"I don't like hearts," JJ said, shoving me off the chair and snagging the seat for himself. "Buddy Blobs! Get your Buddy Blobs!"

I grabbed one of the legs of his chair and tipped him over.

"Get your ugly blob," I called to the nearest kid. JJ stood and dusted himself off. "I don't want to sell lovely hearts!" he said, as he picked me up and carried me out of the chair. He went to gently set me on the cold floor, but I twisted and rolled until we both crashed down.

We were laughing so hard, I was crying. He was holding his belly.

When he got up again, he sprinted to the sales table and took my seat, shouting to passing kids, "Get a Cupid Card. These are way *cuter* than those weird-looking Buddy Blobs!"

"What?" I laughed even harder. He was selling my hearts after all. I shoved him but he didn't budge. He was glued to my chair, and when I went to sit in the blob sales seat, JJ reached out and hugged me.

That was unexpected! But I didn't hate it. I didn't know what to do, though, so I didn't really do anything. I ended up just kind of awkwardly flailing my arms, half around him and half wiggling in the air. I could feel my face heating up.

The hug, thankfully, was interrupted by a kid passing by, who slammed his hand on our table as he went. "This is rockin'!" He was wearing his own handmade HLL t-shirt and screaming for the band like they were famous, performing at a stadium.

I tried to forget the awkward hug, and my weird response, while I sold a girl Buddy Blobs for her entire science class and all her teachers. When she walked away, and the table was quiet for a second, JJ leaned over and said, "Can I ask you something?"

"Sure," I said. I figured he wanted me to handle his "customer" while he grabbed his lunch tray. I'd brought a brown bag, knowing it would be crazy in the cafeteria, but he hadn't thought ahead.

"Will you meet me in the park after school?"

"I—" What was this about? I wanted to know more, but we had a small rush of buyers and JJ really did need to go get lunch before they ran out of tater tots, so I said, "Sure," and watched him walk away.

I was intrigued. It would have to be a fast meeting, though. I couldn't stay in the park too long because I had a date with a surly dog.

Marley walked me to the park. She was massaging her wrists.

"I've never played so hard in my whole life," she said, smiling so wide her lips practically touched her ears. She made some motions with her hands as if playing again. "Ohhh, that hurts . . ." she said, smiling even wider. "It's a good hurt."

"You were fantastic!" I said. "What an amazing first gig! And we sold too many cards to count."

It was time to work on delivery. Olivia said she'd come over on Saturday to organize what we'd sold, sort them into boxes for the fourth period classes, and assign students to deliver them to teachers.

Some kids from the student council had agreed to join us, too.

JJ swore he'd be there, though he said he would be late because of something with his mom. He said he had an idea on how to sell even more cards on Valentine's Day.

Marley said she'd come over to help total up the money we'd earned, which I thought was a lot.

"I saw that hug JJ gave you," Marley said as we turned the corner toward the park.

"I don't remember that," I said, totally lying. I hadn't stopped thinking about it all day. Maybe it was an accident and that's what he wanted to talk about? Maybe he was going to apologize? Maybe he wanted to hug again? What would I do then? I'd need to react better. In or out, not halfway.

Confusing.

"He's going to admit he likes you, finally," Marley said, sure of herself. "He sent that mysterious Buddy Blob and now he'll ask if you want to hang out."

"Hang out?" I laughed. "Is that what you and Rotem are doing?"

"Yes." She nodded. "We're hanging."

I chuckled. Then I had to consider, would I want to "hang out" with JJ if he asked?

"I still hate him," I said to Marley, but my tone was unconvincing.

"Sure," she snorted. "And I'm a royal princess."

"Oh fine," I admitted. "I don't hate him, but it's frustrating that he still has never apologized for the whole science fair thing." I knew it was a long time ago, but it still bothered me.

"True," Marley agreed, pointing across the park. "So when he asks you to be his valentine, you can ask him to explain what happened that day."

"You make it sound so easy . . ." I said. Then I realized that I'd forgotten to tell her something. "Hey," I said, "the other day, Olivia said that she thought I've had a crush on JJ since fourth grade and that I was mad when they started 'going out.' Isn't that crazy? She's got it all wrong."

"Does she?" Marley said.

"What do you mean by that?" I asked.

"Well, yes, Olivia took sides with JJ," Marley said,

"but it wasn't her fault that JJ threw you out of the science project."

There was a tension growing between us, and I wished I hadn't started it.

Marley continued. "Think back, Suki. We were all besties. When did that change?"

I wasn't sure. "When JJ ditched me?"

"You're ridiculous." She shook her head. "You really are a baby sometimes. Don't you remember? You were mad at Olivia before that. In fact, she had been talking about working with JJ for science fair, until you went to school early and signed up to be his partner."

I, for sure, did not remember that. "Why did I do that?"

"Maybe you should ask yourself," Marley said. "Why did you do that?"

"You think I wanted to get between Olivia and JJ because I had a crush on him?" I spluttered. "No way."

She shrugged.

"No way!" I told Marley, my voice rising. "How can you even think that I had a crush on him? You are the worst friend for even thinking that. Haven't I hated him all this time?" She shrugged again and I could practically hear her saying, "There's a thin line between love and hate." She'd been saying that about me and JJ since . . . well, since fourth grade!

I got mad. Madder at my best friend than I'd ever been before. "I can't believe you are taking Olivia's side after all this time! I can't believe you think I wanted to be partners with JJ because I liked him. I can guarantee that if Olivia had done the project with him, then I'd have that ribbon and she'd have been the one with the three-year grudge!" I was on a roll. "If you think I had a crush, then you aren't the friend I thought you were."

That came out a little harsher than I intended. But she just didn't get it. Just because she liked Rotem and he liked her back didn't mean that she knew everything about everyone's crushes. Just like I always thought—boys make everything a mess!

Marley stared at me for a beat. Then, without a word, she rotated on her heel and left the park.

I saw JJ waiting for me in the middle of the park with Sandy. "Hey!" he called, as I approached.

"Hey," I said, still feeling bad about how things had just gone with Marley. I tried to shake it off and pretend I hadn't just started a fight with my best friend. "What did you want to tell me?"

"I have a question," he said.

I tilted my head. This was it. Marley was right—he was going to ask me out. My heart started pounding. I bent down to pet Sandy so I wouldn't have to look at him, and said, "This sounds interesting. Go on." Since working at the shelter, I always had treats in my pocket now. I let her sniff my coat until she found them, then I told her to sit, and gave her one when she did it.

"You're so good with her," JJ said.

I smiled.

"So, can you babysit?" JJ asked me.

"Huh?" I stood to face him. "I thought you were an only child, like me."

He let out a small laugh. "I meant for Sandy."

"Huh?" I was super confused.

"My question was, can you watch Sandy while I'm gone?"

Oh. That was not what I expected. I hated to admit it, but I was a little disappointed.

JJ went on. "I was going to ask if you could dog-sit her just tonight, but then Mom texted me at school to say our plans changed—her weekend thing is now two days, not just one, and I can't take Sandy. So we need to find someone for the whole weekend." There was a desperate tone to his voice. "Olivia's parents are super busy this weekend, so she can't take her, either."

"That stinks," I said.

"There's more: Since it's two nights instead of one, I also have to miss meeting up with the council at your house." He frowned. "I tried to get out of going, but my mom said no. It's like that sometimes. She tells me what to do, and I don't have a choice. So I do it."

I grunted. I mean, I understood when parents laid down the law, but this seemed a little crazy.

"So can you watch Sandy for me?" he finished. "I'll come get her Sunday."

I looked down at the puppy. She was so cute, lying in the grass at our feet. It was a little cold out, but she didn't care. Her orange fur blew in the breeze as she nibbled on a stick. I bent down and took it away. "It's not good to eat sticks," I said. If Sandy could talk, I'm sure she'd have argued with me.

Sandy rose, ready to fetch the stick if I threw it, and that made me wonder if I could train her a little more, maybe get her to fetch and come when called. I'd have the whole weekend to try out what I learned in the training class at the shelter on Sandy. That would be fun!

Having to give her up again would be tough, but if I knew she was well-trained, and JJ agreed, maybe I could dog-sit again sometime!

"I'll ask my parents," I said, head full of happy thoughts and ambitious plans. Fingers crossed they'd say yes, since it was an emergency.

"Great," JJ said. "If they agree, I can bring her over right away. You're a lifesaver, Suki." He checked his phone. "*Ack.* Mom's called four times. I think she wants to leave, like, now."

I said, "Hang on. I'll call my parents and maybe I can take her from here."

While he called his mom, I called mine. No answer. I tried Dad, but no answer there, either.

I really wanted to take care of Sandy! I didn't want JJ to find someone else to do it.

"What did they say?" JJ asked me, when he got off the phone.

I didn't hesitate. "Yes."

"Really?"

Did he sense something was up? I bit my bottom lip and said, "They totally think I am responsible, since I've been working at the shelter, and they think it's good for me to practice with a dog this weekend." Oh what a hole I was digging! I couldn't back out now. "I'll come get her stuff from your place now."

"Thanks, Suki." And in a blink he was leading Sandy around the bushes that divided his apartment complex and the park.

A few minutes later, I was holding a bag of dog things and a leash with a dog at the end of it.

As I put Sandy in an empty cage at the shelter for the afternoon, I realized that I was still disappointed that JJ's question for me had just been about Sandy. But I shook it away, reminding myself that I didn't like him. And didn't want a boyfriend.

I mean, who needed a valentine when I had Sandy to hang out with?

I kept an eye on her while she settled into some old towels I'd put down for a bed. She spun around twice, then dug a spot in the middle of the pile and snuggled up. To make sure no one mistook her for a stray, I put a sign on the cage that said *NOT FOR ADOPTION*, then started my work of filling dog bowls.

I couldn't wait to tell my parents that I was taking care of . . .

Oh, hang on.

Telling them probably wasn't a great idea anymore.

I looked over at Sandy, who looked back up at me with those adorable golden eyes.

After a long breath, I muttered out loud, "This could be a problem."

The right thing to do in this situation would be to call Mom and Dad again immediately and explain what happened.

But it was too late. I already had Sandy with me. What would I say?

Second choice: I wouldn't tell them. Sandy could live in my room. We'd sneak out for walks.

Yeah. That was not the smartest idea, but it felt like the right one. It would be okay. I could hide her for two nights.

"Good girl, Sandy," I called over to her as I slowly entered Bowzer's cage. "Tonight, I'll teach you to fetch."

Chapter Sixteen
IN THE DOG HOUSE

Friday night

My mom reads minds. My dad has supersonic hearing.

I hadn't even been home an hour when they barged into my room. There was no time to hide the evidence.

Dog toys were all over the floor. Treats were on my bedside table. And even though I threw a blanket over Sandy, she became a wiggly lump that made a high-pitched squeaking sound. Kinda obvious.

"Care to explain?" my father asked. He seemed somehow paler than usual. I swear, if the guy didn't get outside soon, he'd become a vampire. I told him that.

"Suki!" His pale face got a little pink. "Do not distract me. The mayor just called to check in on Sandy."

Oh. They didn't have superpowers after all.

"Imagine my surprise when I told her I didn't know what she was talking about!" Dad pinned me with a "You are in so much trouble" gaze. I'd only seen that look once before. It was scary.

"I told her to come get the dog," Dad said.

I gasped and jumped off my bed, knocking my pillow down.

Sandy crept out from the covers to see what was going on. She looked at me with pathetic eyes, as if she knew she was leaving.

"No. Dad!" I turned to face my mom. "Mom, please. I promised JJ. I can handle it. I really can. I'll show you!"

"You should have asked us," Mom said, in a low voice. She never raised her voice or got mad anymore. It was almost worse that she spoke without obvious emotion.

"I know." I put a hand out to steady Sandy and keep her from jumping off the bed. "And I did call, you just didn't answer. But he needed someone right away, and it all just happened so fast. Please, don't send her home." I was full-on crying now. Sandy, sensing something was terribly wrong, licked my hand. I scooped her into my arms. "Please . . ."

"The mayor can't come back until Sunday," my dad said.

I felt a catch in my throat and swallowed a breath. My tears were flowing and I wiped them on my sleeve.

Mom stepped forward. "Suki, you must do exactly as you promised. You'll take care of Sandy until Sunday afternoon."

"And after that," Dad said, "you're grounded."

"What does that mean?" I asked, relieved that I was keeping Sandy.

"You'll go to school. Come home. Do homework. No TV. No phone. No hanging out at Marley's. You'll be grounded for three weeks." Dad was firm.

Mom nodded. "One week for each day you thought you'd try to trick us."

When my parents made a decision together, they never backed down. It was probably some parenting strategy they'd read about. So being grounded for three rotten weeks was not going to change. I knew it was stupid to argue, but still, there was one big detail to consider, so I said, "I have a job at the shelter. I have to go tomorrow."

Mom and Dad looked at each other, passing secret messages through their eyes. They'd clearly forgotten about the shelter.

"We'll discuss it," Mom said at last.

"Take that dog out to the yard," Dad instructed before the two of them backed out of the room. "If she messes in the house, I'll be furious."

The door shut behind them.

My tears stopped. Three weeks grounding was way too much, but I'd take it. I still could work at the shelter . . . probably.

I grabbed a leash and took Sandy to go potty, then started the training I'd been planning.

I decided to follow the videos and start with "Sit" and "Stay," just like the Dog-Talker suggested, even though by now I knew he was pretty much a fraud. He did still work with dogs, so even if they were further along than he let on when the cameras started rolling, he'd trained them, right?

Tomorrow, I would add "Come" and work on "Heel." Maybe we'd cover "Fetch" on Sunday morning.

Standing outside in my tiny backyard, with a poop bag in one hand and a treat in the other, I realized I'd forgotten to tell my parents that the student council was coming over in the morning to get ready for delivering Valentine's Day Cupid Cards. They couldn't cancel that, right? Mom had already said that student council commitments were important. I could remind her of that, if I had to.

I'd messed up. I knew that, and I wished I'd asked my parents before I brought Sandy home. But I also had the most adorable, best dog ever living in my room for the weekend. So things weren't all bad.

Well, I mean except for what happened with Marley. At least I had Cinnamon Bun to distract me.

Sunday morning, the doorbell rang, and my dad answered it. He was wearing a suit and had his suit-case packed for a conference.

When he looked outside, Olivia was standing on the porch, holding a bag of extra supplies. She clearly had not heard about my fight with Marley.

"I forgot to tell you," I said, pushing past my dad to let her in. It had been a long night. Sandy had cried a lot. She was confused about where she was, and needed to go out in the middle of the night. I didn't sleep well. I wished I'd thought to have a crate. Crate training was key, and I was breaking every rule.

"Elizabeth!" Dad shouted over his shoulder. Clearly, this was not something he wanted to deal with on his own.

"Bruce?" My mom came to the door just as four other people from student council arrived.

My dad looked at her. Mom looked at me. Then, reluctantly, they stepped aside to let everyone in.

While kids scooted past and went up to my room, Dad whispered, "Still grounded."

"I know," I replied. Just because it was awkward already, I tossed out, "Can you order pizza?"

With a huge sigh, Dad said, "Yes, but only cheese," as if that was the punishment.

I smiled. "Thanks." Spontaneously, I hugged each of my parents and, with Sandy nipping at my heels, rushed upstairs to get to work.

Marley never showed up. It felt weird trying to do all the Cupid Cards stuff without her.

Still, the volunteers were getting a lot done and were ready for a break when JJ called on video chat, to explain his idea for increasing sales.

I had expected him to call, but I didn't expect him to be mad.

"Let's get to work." That was the first thing he said. No "Hey" or "Hi" or "How's it goin'?"

I could feel his anger through the computer screen. That's how furious he was. I wanted to say, "Get in line," since Marley was mad at me, too. I was feeling bitter and down, so I overcompensated by being cheery.

"I have Sandy right here," I said, picking her up and sticking her little face into the camera. "She's good."

"You got me in trouble with my mom," JJ announced, as if the rest of the room wasn't listening. "She said I tricked her."

"I—" It was sort of true. He'd asked and I said okay and he handed me everything right away. "Well, what would you have done if I'd said no?" I countered.

"I'd have found someone else—" It was his turn to stall. "Well, maybe. But that's not the point," JJ said at last. I couldn't see what he was wearing, but at the top of his neck it looked like he had a collared shirt and maybe a suit on. Wherever he was with his mom must have been fancy. He said, "You should have told me that you couldn't take her."

"I wanted to do it," I said, putting Sandy down.

She seemed confused that JJ's voice was in the room but he wasn't here at the same time. Her cute little head was spinning around, searching for him. Seeing her look for him made me annoyed. JJ didn't deserve her.

I pointed at the screen, but Sandy didn't understand.

"What's the problem?" I asked JJ. "I'm grounded, but it all worked out." I knew he wouldn't be mad anymore when he saw everything I'd taught Sandy. She'd learned to roll over this morning. I was saving it for a surprise when he got back.

JJ grunted something. Not sure what, but it sounded rude. I wondered if he was grounded, too.

This whole thing reminded me that JJ and I weren't really ever friends. He'd still never apologized or explained about the incident in fourth grade, and here he was, being all ridiculous again. I was the one who he ditched back then, and I was the one in trouble now, thanks to him. If anyone was supposed to be mad, it should be me.

I was about to get into it with him, when Olivia gently pushed me out of the camera range.

"JJ, you want to get to work, so let's do it," she said. "How are we going to deliver fifteen hundred candy cards in one day?"

Suddenly, there was a ding on everyone's phones at the same time.

"I just texted you," he said. Then, without another word to me or anyone else, JJ logged off the call.

"That was weird," I said. "What's up with him?"

"I don't have a clue." Olivia shrugged and went to grab her phone. "This is bad," she reported. "Super-duper bad."

Everyone in my room started complaining as they stared at their screens.

The message JJ had sent us all was short and clear.

I quit.

Chapter Seventeen
LESSONS LEARNED

Sunday, February 13—One day to go!

Sunday afternoon, JJ's mom came to get Sandy. I peeked out the window at her car while she talked softly with my parents in the kitchen. If JJ was behind those shaded car windows, I couldn't see him.

There was no way to show him everything I'd taught Sandy. And that was a huge disappointment because she needed practice. I'd set the base for her training, but she needed to be worked with every day to make sure she could follow commands.

I decided to text him about it.

Then I changed my mind.

He'd totally built up this great idea for selling more Candy Cards and getting them all delivered, but then he didn't come through. He quit when we needed him. Why should I help him or his dog?

Then I changed my mind again. She was a great dog. It was just that JJ was a bad dude.

Oh, I was confused. In the end, the dog won my heart, so I texted.

Commands Sandy knows:

Sit, stay, come, leave it, fetch, and shake.

Practice with her.

I remembered something he'd really like and added:

She likes soccer.

That was from the first day I'd met Sandy in the park.

In the end, I'd sent four texts, but didn't the dog deserve it? If I ever dog-sat for her again, I'd teach her that Cinnamon Bun was her name. Ha! That would show JJ. Then again, there was no chance I'd ever dog-sit her—or probably even see her—again.

My heart sank at that thought. I decided to go early to the shelter. There was another dog that I wanted to see—Bowzer.

I waited until Sandy was gone, threw on my shirt, and headed out.

"Suki, wait up," Olivia called out in a way that made me wonder if she'd been standing in her driveway watching for me. She'd probably just gotten home from dog training. I'd had to miss the training class that morning because my parents wanted me home when the mayor came.

"What's up?" I asked her.

"I'm really sorry," she said. Luna was sitting at her feet in a "Stay" position. The training at the shelter really helped. I was happy to see Luna doing so well. Which, of course, made me think about Sandy again.

I sighed.

"What are you sorry for?" I asked her. I mean I sort of knew, but still . . .

"JJ," Olivia said. She pushed a long strand of hair behind her ear.

"I don't blame you that he quit at the last minute," I said.

"I know," she said. "But I should have warned you. After what happened with the dog, his mom grounded him. She made him quit."

Oh. That was too bad.

"I get it," I said. "I am grounded, too. But my parents made me honor my commitments." I added, "And I'm glad they did."

"JJ's mom isn't like that." Olivia looked over her shoulder. Even though we were at my house, she looked back at her own as if someone was listening. Then, seeming confident that we were alone, Olivia whispered, "Look, I know how fast you get mad sometimes, so I shouldn't tell you this, but it really *is* science fair all over again."

I seriously had no idea what Olivia was talking about. "And you should know, we were never really dating . . . his plan backfired."

Huh? I started to ask what she meant, when Olivia said, "I gotta go."

"Wait, Olivia—"

"Bye, Suki," she said loudly. "See you at the meeting place an hour before school tomorrow." And with that, she commanded, "Luna, heel," and Luna walked right next to her left leg, into the house.

The conversation was weird, and any joy I felt from watching Luna behave so well was tempered by what she'd said. What did she mean that it was science fair all over again . . . and did she just say I got mad fast? What? That wasn't my own impression of me.

I stopped to think about her words.

Did I get mad fast?

I guessed maybe I did.

It was possible that I also didn't always stop to hear the other side of an argument . . . and I held on to grudges forever.

Maybe I should just hang out with dogs instead of people.

I looked forward to getting to the shelter. Animal feelings were much more straightforward than human feelings.

"Hi," I said to Mrs. Ryan as I walked past her on the way to the back room. "Since it's quiet, can I take Bowzer into the training room?" There was an idea I had that I wanted to try.

She looked at me and pressed her lips together. "You've made progress with him," she said, "but I'm not sure he'll ever be ready for much more." Mrs. Ryan pushed up her glasses. "Look, Suki, I know how hard you're trying with him, but it's still going to be hard to find someone to adopt him."

"You don't know what will happen," I countered. I was determined to make him lovable.

"I've been working here a long time," she replied. I could see the sadness behind her eyes. "But it's likely we'll have to close soon. We're adopting out as many pets as we can, but not replacing them," she told me. "New strays are going to other shelters in other cities." Mrs. Ryan gave a sorry breath and pushed her glasses up again, even though they hadn't slid down. "Seeing the band play was great. Your fund-raising idea is fantastic, but I'm afraid it won't be enough. I've made peace with closing, Suki."

I wanted to argue. But she was right. Whatever we ended up donating from the Candy Cards would only be a few hundred dollars—it was just a Band-Aid for a gigantic wound. We might be able to stop the blood gushing for a little while, but there'd be more problems after that.

"Maybe you kids should put the money you earn back into a fancy school dance," Mrs. Ryan told me.

I shook my head. "No," I said. "The final day of the Cupid Cards fund-raiser is tomorrow, and people want to help the shelter. We've already raised a lot of money and there will be more coming in." I tried to feel positive when I added, "Maybe something extra-awesome will happen." In the meantime, I was going ahead as if the shelter would always be here and stay open. "I'd still really like to work with Bowzer in the big room today," I said.

Mrs. Ryan gave in. "All right," she said. "But if you feel like he's not handling things well, you must leave the room and lock him inside."

"Of course!" I agreed.

Bowzer was a stubborn dog. He let me pet him, and he let me put on a collar and leash, but when I said, "Come," he lay down.

But I was stubborn, too. I put my hands bravely around his belly and dragged/lifted him back up to his feet. All those treats I was giving him were making him heavy. And he was already huge to start with. At least he was eating . . .

"Come," I said again when Bowzer started to slip down to the floor. I tugged the leash and convinced him to stay standing.

"Come," I said again, and this time, he reluctantly waddled along with me toward the training room.

Most dogs walk faster than their owners and the

owners get dragged along, but not Bowzer. He moved so slowly, we could have been going backward. Progress was slow, but I was patient. I figured as long as he was calm, I'd let him set the pace.

When we got to the room, I finally gave him his first treat.

I hadn't set anything out in the room. No toys or balls or obstacle course things to go over or under. It was just me, Bowzer, and a big empty space. I wasn't in any hurry.

"Let's start with 'Sit,'" I told the monster. He looked at me. Snorted. Yawned. And flopped to the ground.

I sighed.

"Come on," I went for honesty. "If you don't get your lazy bones up, no one will want you. I'm working hard to make sure this place doesn't close. But even if it doesn't, it's up to you to get adopted. So get up off the floor and help me out!"

I don't know if he understood or not, but Bowzer slowly rose. His tail wagged faster than I'd ever seen it and when I said, "Sit," again . . . that lump of a dog sat!

"Now we're getting somewhere," I cheered and moved to the next command. "Stay!"

Finally! Bowzer's prior training was coming back.

As I played with Bowzer, I had to admit how much I'd actually learned from the Dog-Talker show. Yes, his dogs were trained already, but so was Bowzer. When I thought back on each episode, I could see how to use that fact. Once I got Bowzer to "remember" his first commands, others came pretty easy.

I think all that dog needed was some love. And I had plenty to give.

Time passed quickly. I needed to leave soon, so I was going through all the commands with Bowzer one more time.

"Sit," I said. That lump of a dog put his tush on the ground and stared up at me.

"Down," I told Bowzer, and pointed to the ground. There was a moment when I thought he couldn't handle it. He gave me this eye roll, like I do when my parents ask me to clear the dinner table, but then, he did the task. He lay down in his usual "I'm a dog-carpet" pose.

I wondered . . . could he roll over?

Tucking a meaty treat into my palm, I put my hand close enough so Bowzer could smell it, then I moved my whole hand in a wide circle. The idea was, he would smell the treat, roll over, and get the treat.

Bowzer smelled my hand and bared his teeth. "Don't do that," I told him, and he seemed to relax.

"Roll over," I said, again, waving my palm around in a circle.

It seemed like he was laughing at me. He snorted and put his head on the floor by my knee.

"Come on," I begged. "I know you can do it. How are you going to get adopted if you refuse to even try things? I bet you rolled over a thousand times for your old family. Show me so I can tell your new family how awesome you are!"

Bowzer yawned.

Oh well. I guess he didn't want to roll over today. "Come," "Sit," and "Down" were a good start. I wouldn't push it.

"Done for today," I told Bowzer. "You can go nap in your cage." I gave him the treat in my hand and he gobbled it up.

I stepped back. "Come," I commanded. I smacked a hand on the side of my leg. "Come," I repeated, pulling on his leash.

Hmmm . . . this was a problem. What was I going to

do if he refused to go back to his cage? What would I tell Mrs. Ryan if I had to get her to help me? It would be a total failure.

"Give me a break here, Bowzer," I muttered as my frustration grew.

Was he playing with me? I had a feeling the dog knew exactly what was going on. With a small "Woof," he looked right at me, rolled that heavy body over, and finally got up.

"Oh, Bowzer," I cooed. "You know more than you are telling me." I was so happy, I bent down and gave him a big hug around the neck.

He licked the side of my face.

Through the window into the training room, I saw Ben standing outside, giving me a thumbs-up.

It was such a good morning that I couldn't let the rest of the day drag me down. I had to talk to Marley.

When I knocked on her door, her mom said, "Hi, Suki. Let me go check on Marley—wait here." Clearly, she knew what had happened between us—I don't think she'd ever checked in with Marley before letting me inside.

"Come on, she's in the garage," Marley's mom said

a minute later. She pointed the way, as if it was my first visit there.

Marley was sitting on a stool, messing around on Rotem's bass. She didn't look up when I came in.

I jumped right into it. "I'm sorry."

She didn't say anything, just kept playing.

"Seriously, Marley, I am so sorry."

"I know you are," she said after a long pause. "And you know I can never stay mad at you."

I sighed. "It's me that holds all the grudges," I said.

"Yep," she agreed, putting aside the guitar and coming over to me. "But it's not like that's new information." She put her arm around me. "You're still my bestie."

I smiled. "Forever," I said.

Marley walked back to her stool and sat. I took another chair to face her.

"I am thinking that I need to slow things down." Ah man, I sounded like my mom! As long as I was going that route, I should dive in. "Maybe be a little more mindful before I get mad about stuff."

"I have literally no idea what that means," Marley said. "How about you just ask to hear the other side first before jumping to conclusions?"

"Okay." I gave a small laugh. We sat in silence for a long moment, then I said, "So, what happened with the science fair?"

"You should ask JJ," Marley told me.

I gave her a look, which meant I wasn't going to and she should just tell me.

"Oh, fine." She gave in. "JJ's dad was moving out. It was the last weekend before he left town. Permanently." As Marley said that, I sort of remembered. "His dad saw the pieces of the car and wanted to help JJ build it. JJ didn't have the heart to tell him you two were supposed to do it together."

"It was his last chance to do something with his dad?"

"Yeah, remember, he moved and after that JJ only saw him at holidays."

I did remember that. Right after his dad left, his mom threw herself into politics. JJ never talked about where his dad went and, in time, I think he stopped going to visit—I'm not even sure where his dad lived.

"Well, his mom was so upset that they'd made the car without you, since it was supposed to be a team project, she made JJ call the school and tell them what happened."

"My dad had to call the teacher too . . ."

"I'm pretty sure someone would have called you to explain if you'd waited longer," Marley said. "That's what my mom said."

I guess I did move too quickly sometimes. I was the one who made my dad call right away to tell the teacher I'd be working alone. Oh good grief.

"But how did JJ win the blue ribbon if his dad helped?" I asked, feeling the anger start to rise in me again. But then I stopped myself—I was new Suki, not mad Suki.

"Parents were allowed to help in fourth grade. Didn't your dad help with the volcano?"

"Uh, no," I said.

"Hmmm . . . That explains the fire." She bit her bottom lip and tapped her toe to a beat in her head. "I didn't even know what really happened with JJ until a few days ago when my mom told me."

"Why'd she tell you?" I asked.

"She saw us trying to get Luna and asked me why we never played with Olivia anymore."

"Play?" I nearly laughed.

"Whatever. I guess I had never told her, or she didn't realize what happened, but when I explained, she filled me in on the other side," Marley said. "Olivia stuck with JJ 'cause she knew how important making that car was to him."

"But then *you* never told me what happened . . ." I started to feel that familiar anger rise again. "This could have been so different!"

"Could it?" Marley asked me. "If you wanted to know what happened that day, you'd have asked. It's been three years. The ball was on your side of the field, Suki. You never kicked it." She added, "Of course, you're not alone. I didn't ask anyone, either . . ."

It was all true. We both felt awful about it.

All those years, I'd had this huge competitive streak with JJ, and I didn't even know why it started. I wish I'd known about his dad and the car.

My stomach hurt thinking about it. But as dumb as it sounded, there was a reason I never let him explain. It was time I admitted it to myself.

Here's the truth . . .

I *did* have a huge crush on JJ in fourth grade. And the more we worked together, the worse it got.

In the end, it was easier for me to get mad and run away than to really listen to him. *Augh*.

Admitting that was hard. Even harder than

getting stitches or training Bowzer! Or even asking Mrs. Choi if JJ and I could work together on the Cupid Cards after all. Whoever said that middle school is the hardest years was so right!

"Hey," Marley said, interrupting my thoughts. "One more thing—JJ never really 'dated' Olivia."

"Olivia told me that . . ." I didn't understand when she said it, but now it was clear. "He wanted me to be jealous! Oh, Marley! JJ *wanted* me to go ask to be his partner for the project!" I couldn't believe it. "JJ had a crush on me in fourth grade."

Marley nodded and laughed. "Smarter than you look."

I didn't feel very smart, but still, I was figuring things out.

When Olivia said it "was science fair all over again" she didn't mean he was planning to do another project without me.

No.

She meant: JJ liked me!

Chapter Eighteen
IT ALL COMES DOWN TO THIS

It's here! It's Monday, February 14! It's Valentine's Day!!!

"If this mess ends up on the Internet, I might die," I told Marley. First period was coming to an end and we had a box full of cards that hadn't been sorted for fourth period delivery.

"You won't die," Marley said, standing over me. Her hair blocked the lights in the hall. "No one ever died from embarrassment."

"I'll be the first." I was lying on the ground, staring at the ceiling. "What are we going to do?" I moaned.

There was no way to get all those cards delivered. When JJ quit, so did his team of helpers. We tried to replace everyone, but the entire soccer team left with JJ. Without more volunteers, we were doomed.

We'd planned to sell even more cards at lunch. If we couldn't deliver the ones we already had sorted, how could we add more to the pile? As it was, we'd already been up past midnight trying to get it all done. When parents came to my house to pick up kids, we agreed to meet early. So without much sleep, here we were!

"We sold too many cards. I knew this would happen." I closed my eyes and imagined all the cards neatly sorted and organized.

When I opened them again, the piles of red hearts and candy sticks were still there, all jumbled up!

This was a disaster.

Maybe I just wouldn't come to school the rest of the week. That wouldn't solve anything, but at least I wouldn't be there when everyone was demanding their money back.

"I'm here to save the day," Rotem said, marching into the large classroom that the student council had taken over as Candy Cards headquarters.

"No one can save us now." I moped.

"I brought troops," Rotem said, opening the door. JJ was standing in the hall.

"Can we volunteer?" JJ asked, stepping aside to show the soccer players behind him.

New, not-quick-to-anger Suki had a fight with old, mad, and scrappy Suki in my head. New Suki won. "What are you doing here?" I asked in a calm voice. But I couldn't help muttering, "You quit and took all your big ideas with you. It's your fault that this disaster will be a meme by tonight."

"I'm here now," JJ told me. "We're going to sort the old cards fast and get ready to sell new ones at lunch." He moved into the room with his friends, pushing me aside.

I stalked after him. "We can't sell any more cards," I said. "Seriously. We've maxed out."

"Don't be such a *bummer*, Suki," JJ teased me. "More sales means more money for the shelter."

His friends mixed in with the few council members in the room. Hearts and blobs were practically flying across the room from the unsorted piles into their designated classroom boxes.

"I'm not a bummer—" I began, when the door to the sorting room opened.

It was Principal Hollis. He was a big guy, built like a truck, with eyes like darts.

"Who's in trouble?" Rotem asked softly.

"Must be JJ for letting all these soccer players skip class," I said.

"I have permission," JJ reminded me.

The principal's eyes met mine and locked. "Ah shoot, it's me!" I said. "I wonder what I did."

Once he'd found me, the principal marched over with determined steps. Behind him, I saw two people. One with a microphone and one with a camera.

"It's *Channel Five News!*" Marley told me. "Check my hair." She was panicking. "Does it look okay?"

It was a trick question that I couldn't answer. It looked like it always did. Gigantic and fluffy.

"Pretty," Rotem said, and JJ and I spun around to look at him.

"What?" he said. "It's pretty." He glanced at his shoes.

I wondered how many Cupid Cards Marley would get from Rotem today. I hoped a lot. Over the past couple days, I had realized that a boyfriend didn't necessarily mean the end of a friendship. I was rooting for them to figure that out, too.

"I'm Veronica Sanchez," the woman with the microphone said, pushing past our principal to get to our table first. She was shorter than she seemed on TV. She was wearing TV clothes: a short skirt and a blazer. Perfect lipstick. "I'm from the local news."

"We know!" Marley said so loudly I thought I heard an echo. "My mom watches you all the time!"

"I'm flattered," Veronica Sanchez replied. She glanced around at each of us. "I saw online that you have sold more than a thousand Cupid Cards. We think that's a local school record."

I looked over at Rotem. I had no idea what he'd uploaded, but it was clearly his talent that got us here. He tipped his head at JJ and I realized what happened.

JJ was the one with the idea to contact the news. He'd said he had a big idea to share at the meeting, but then we both got in trouble about Sandy, and we know how that went. But JJ still did what he'd said. He and Rotem got us—and the shelter—some really awesome publicity.

Veronica nodded to her camera guy. "Gus and I want to interview you for tonight's broadcast," she told us. We all said that was okay, and she held up a microphone. "What are you planning to do with the money you earned?" she asked, then pointed the microphone at me, saying, "A live band for your dance? Balloon arches?"

I shook my head, nervous to be on TV. Luckily, JJ helped me out.

He stood right next to me and leaned in. "It was all Suki's idea," he said, and looked at me encouragingly.

"We're raising money for the animal shelter," I said. "We're still having a regular dance, but we're donating all the extra money we make to the shelter."

JJ added, "The mayor is going help, too. She's announcing our fund-raiser in email blast to the city."

That was a great idea! I don't know how he'd done it, but he'd not only come to help, he'd also gotten his mom on board.

I couldn't help myself. JJ was a better guy than I'd given him credit for. In fact, he was a really great guy.

"I don't know how you got un-grounded, but I'm glad you did," I said. I leaned forward and gave him a huge kiss on the cheek. Right there on TV. I could feel my cheeks burning, but I felt good. As I pulled away, I saw the other students, the camera, and the reporter all staring at us.

"This is good TV," Veronica told Gus. "You're the mayor's son, right?"

"Yep." JJ smiled and touched his cheek, which was a little flushed. He looked up, over the reporter's head at the clock and said, "We gotta go. There's a lot of work to do if we are going to save the shelter."

Veronica glanced at Marley and Rotem and then at me and JJ and asked, "Can we watch this process in action?"

"Only if I can tell you about the shelter while we work," I said, feeling a lot less nervous and much more calm now.

"Of course," she replied. "I'll see what I can do to help, too. Gus adopted a bunny from there last week."

I laughed so hard I snorted. "I wondered who took the bunny!"

"Fluffy Face," Gus said, checking the settings on his camera. "That's his name."

"It fits," I said, smiling.

JJ leaned over to me and said, "I already have some ideas on how to sell even more cards next year!"

I looked around the room, which was slowly getting in shape for delivery. "Like what?" I asked. "How can we ever beat this year?"

"I was thinking about a day where if you buy a card, you can pet Sandy," he said with a laugh.

"She *is* the cutest," I agreed. "Maybe that would wo—"

"We're filming in three . . ." Veronica interrupted, and Gus raised his camera.

Later that evening, I was getting ready to watch the news with my mom and dad. It had been the best day.

"Hang on," I told them. "Don't pause it. I'll be back in time."

I ran next door and rang the bell. Luna barked.

Olivia opened the door. Her eyes were wide, surprised to see me there. Last time we'd talked one-on-one had been weird, but what she'd said had been the spark that made me really think about everything.

"Come over and watch the news with my family," I invited her. "Please."

Even though things were kind of tense between us, she'd been at school early to help sort cards before class, and she came to help deliver boxes to classrooms in fourth period. Olivia was the kind of friend I wanted to be. She stuck by JJ after science fair, but she was never mean to me and Marley (except when she was frustrated by us being mean to her). She didn't get mad and hold a grudge. She wasn't perfect, but still, she seemed darned close.

I decided to totally clear the air. I told her, "I am so

sorry for the past three years! I really want us all to be besties again."

"What?" She seemed a little confused. "Is this just because I told you I was never really dating JJ?"

"No, of course not!" I said. "That was so, so long ago. I just got so swept up in being super competitive with him that I ignored everything else." I sighed. "I really regret it all." I reached out my hand, like a peace offering. "Come over. Let's restart our old friendship."

She considered my hand, and just when I thought Olivia might leave me hanging, she took my hand in hers.

"Finally," she said. She looked at me and smiled.

We ran to my house and got there just in time. The news was starting.

"We're raising money for the animal shelter," I was saying into the camera.

On the screen, Marley popped her head into the frame behind me and said, "Yeah!"

Rotem, JJ, and Olivia all gathered around, too, and JJ gave the newscaster a tour of the room, showing off how many hearts we had to deliver.

"We're selling more at lunch!" Marley blurted out, sticking her head back in the frame.

They showed a little clip of us selling cards after that. Since they couldn't stay for lunch, I sat at the table and Rotem pretended to buy a few hearts and a blob.

Then, it cut to the shelter, where Mrs. Ryan gave a quick tour.

"Hey!" I shouted, when Bowzer came onto the screen. "Look at who's a TV star!" The last of the puppies had been moved to the cage next to him and were yipping for attention. He just looked annoyed, which I thought was adorable.

When it was over, my parents were beaming with pride.

"Ice cream sundaes for everyone!" Dad said.

"I'll get the fudge sauce," Mom said, heading out of the living room and into the kitchen. Mom never ate dessert, but it was a special night and we were going to celebrate.

Before Dad left the room, he whispered to me, "You're growing up so fast, my Pumpkin." I thought I saw his eyes well up, but he turned away too quickly for me to be sure.

I clicked off the TV and started to search my phone to see if someone had uploaded the news clip to the Internet yet. I was sure Rotem was on that.

My phone dinged with a text.

Did you get a Cupid Card from JJ?

It was Marley. I'd been expecting her to ask. We'd just been so busy with cleanup and the TV interview and everything that I'd been able to avoid her long looks and shoulder raises.

She couldn't come over because she'd promised to watch the TV broadcast with her grandma at the retirement home. But I couldn't wait to tell her who *did* come over. Olivia and I took a selfie and sent it to her, and I was pretty sure I could hear her cheering from all the way across town.

Then, I replied:

No card. But that's ok. We were on TV!

I added a whole lot of smiling face emojis after that.

I'd actually gotten a lot of cards. I hadn't taken a good look at them yet, but I'd flipped through earlier to see if one was from JJ. There wasn't.

I had a huge math assignment to do, but first things first. As I signed off with Marley, I took out the bag I'd put the cards in and started to go through them more carefully.

One from Rotem.

One from Marley.

One from my math teacher.

One from each kid on student council.

And a special one from Mrs. Choi.

I'd gotten many hearts, and a few blobs. A lot of them thanked me for helping raise money for the shelter. They all made me feel good! I'd sent out a bunch of cards, too—I hoped everyone felt happy when they got them.

I thought I'd opened all my Cupid Cards. I knew they'd all been delivered, so I was totally surprised to find one had been slipped into my locker the next morning. It was a blob-shaped card and on it, in carefully printed letters, the message said:

Meet me at the park after school.

JJ

Chapter Nineteen
CARDS AND GIFTS

Tuesday, February 15

The last bell rang and I ran out of school. The first person I found in the park was Marley. I couldn't believe it!

"What are you doing here?" I asked.

Marley laughed. "I came to find out if JJ admits to sending you the Valentine's Day card last week!" Marley glanced over at the biggest tree in the park. I saw movement there.

"Is Rotem here, too?" I asked.

"Duh," she said, rolling her eyes at me. "He wouldn't miss this. We have to know what happens."

"I'd have texted . . ."

"Texting takes too long," Marley said, throwing her sweatshirt hood over her hair, as if that would disguise her.

She walked toward Rotem's hiding spot. I should never have told her about JJ's card.

I tried to look busy as I waited, scrolling through videos on my phone, but my heart raced every time I heard the rustle of grass. I'd casually look up and wave to whoever was passing by, as if it was totally normal for me to be in the park, alone, on a chilly afternoon. I'd decided to sit on the bench where it all started. The place I'd first seen Cinnamon Bun. It was cold enough out that my butt was freezing and I had to keep shifting to move my jacket to put a buffer between me and the seat.

I was thinking I should probably go inside somewhere, when I heard the barking.

This time, my heart practically stopped when I saw Sandy running toward me. She was off her leash and heading straight toward the bench.

"Sandy!" I called as she came dashing up. I put up a hand, the symbol for "Sit," and didn't even have to give a verbal command. She sat right away, panting with that cute tongue and looking up at me with happy eyes. What a good dog!

"I'm glad to see you," I gushed, bending down to her level to give her a hug,

"She's happy to see you, too," JJ told me. Then, he added, "Me, too."

I smiled. I was happy to see him, too. I had definitely stopped hating him!

He had a box in his hand. "I know it's a day late, but I got you something for Valentine's Day." He held the small green box toward me.

"Oh," I said, flustered. I'd meant to send him a Cupid Card last week, but then he got all mad at me, and I decided not to put it in with the others. Then I forgot to put it back yesterday when we were okay again. I felt bad. "I—"

"No stress," JJ said. "I'm just so glad we're friends now."

I thought about that. It was true. Somewhere in the middle of all the Cupid Chaos and the Dog-Sitting Disaster, we'd become friends. Good friends. And maybe, just maybe, there was a spark of something more. It wasn't like fourth grade. This was something different. All I knew was that I liked how I felt around JJ.

He pointed at the Valentine's Day gift, which was now sitting beside me on the bench. "Open it," JJ said.

The box wasn't wrapped, so I slipped off the lid and peeked inside.

"A leash?" I declared, untangling a long lead and shaking it out. "But I don't have a dog."

"I'm hoping you can help me with Sandy, and hang out with both of us more," JJ said, just as Sandy rolled over in the grass.

"I'd love to!" I said. Then I thought about it for a moment and added, laughing, "I think I better ask my parents first, though." I put the leash back in the box and stuck it into my backpack.

JJ laughed, too. "Yeah," he agreed. "If I go out of town, ask them, but any other time, just come over . . ."

"I will!" I imagined drinking a cup of Cinnamon Bun Swirl while walking in the park with Sandy . . . and maybe JJ, too. "Thanks," I told him. "I may never get a dog of my own, but this is really close."

"That reminds me," JJ said. "You never did tell me who Cinnamon Bun is. That day, at my apartment, you said your dog was in my yard, but now I know you don't have one."

"I—" Yikes. I really didn't want to explain.

And lucky for me, I didn't have to, because Sandy started barking at the trees where Marley and Rotem were hiding. She was pulling on her leash and making such a huge racket that Marley and Rotem slowly came out into the open.

Sandy seemed proud to have found them.

"Did you know they were there the whole time?" JJ asked me.

I replied simply, "No matter what I do, I can't shake them."

JJ rolled his eyes and said, "Hey," to Marley and Rotem. "Do you often hang out in bushes spying on people?"

"Sometimes," Rotem confessed.

At that, JJ looked worried.

"I'm joking," Rotem told him.

We all laughed.

"Marley wants to know about this." From my jeans' back pocket, I pulled out the anonymous Buddy Blob that had fallen from my locker. "Did you give it to me?"

He shook his head. "No, I didn't send you that, Suki." There was a serious look in his eyes. "Honestly, I forgot to send you one, and then when it was time, I was mad at you."

"Same," I told him.

"So I got you the leash instead of a card."

I wished that I'd thought to get him a gift. I asked, "If you didn't put the Buddy Blob into my locker, who did?" I stood up and looked around the park.

Rotem sheepishly raised his hand. "Oops. That was me." He looked at the blob and took it from me. "Looks like I put it in the wrong locker. I would have explained sooner, if I'd known." Rotem blushed. "I didn't understand why Marley wasn't trying to figure out who sent her a mysterious card." He turned to Marley, took the card from me, and handed it to her. "It was supposed to be for you."

"Oh, that's so cute!" Marley said, holding it to her chest. "Thanks, Rotem." She added, "I was hoping to get one from you, but figured you were just too busy thinking of some new invention or song lyrics or something."

"What the heck, Rotem, you bought a *blob*?" I acted like I was insulted.

"I like pizza," Rotem said. "It was an early purchase."

I rolled my eyes.

A few minutes later, I saw Ben running over toward us through the park.

"Hey! Suki, I've been looking everywhere for you!" he said. He was still wearing his backpack from school, but was carrying his coat so I could see his shelter volunteer t-shirt. "Come on. We need to get to the shelter. There's something there you have to see."

Chapter Twenty
The Best Day

Tuesday, February 15, Continued

"Surprise!" Mrs. Ryan greeted me and my friends at the shelter door. She was standing in a way that blocked the glass and made it impossible to see inside. "Suki." She pulled me in for a hug. "None of this would have happened without you."

What? I was confused!

She hugged Marley and Rotem, too. I'd forgotten she knew them from Happy Little Llamas. Then she turned to JJ, who was standing a little way back.

"I heard what you all did to help the shelter," she said. "Your mom's a good mayor, and you are a great citizen." Before he knew what was happening, Mrs. Ryan grabbed JJ and gave him a hug that was bigger and longer than she'd given any of the rest of us.

When she let him go, he looked completely confused. Which was still how I felt.

I asked Ben, "What's going on?"

"Since the news yesterday, with the story about the Cupid Cards and you guys helping the shelter, plus the mayor's newsletter, the phone hasn't stopped ringing." Ben imitated a phone buzzing. "I'm not kidding. I wasn't sure we'd ever get to sleep. Mom and I were here really late."

"Come inside," Mrs. Ryan said, stepping away from the shelter door.

I could now see through the glass. The front area around the desk was packed with people. And, to my even greater surprise, when I walked in my mom and dad were the first to congratulate me.

"Mrs. Ryan called this morning," Mom told me. "She invited us to this celebration."

"What are we celebrating?" I was seriously unclear what was going on. I mean, we'd ended up raising about a thousand dollars for the shelter at school, but that wasn't nearly enough to keep it open forever. I was just hoping it could last a little while longer, and maybe help bring back the vet a few times.

"Hi!" Olivia rushed up and hugged me. Luna was with her. She barked playfully. Olivia told Luna to "Sit," which she did. "Did you see it?" Olivia asked.

"See what?"

"Suki, look!" Olivia pointed at a banner hanging behind the desk. The area was so crowded, I'd missed it. It said:

The Shelter Welcomes our New Sponsors

And below that were the names of about ten different businesses in town, including the yoga studio my mom worked at.

"What does this mean?" I asked Olivia, not quite processing everything. The noise, the people, my parents . . . what was going on?

Before she could answer, Mrs. Ryan called for everyone's attention. She was standing on a chair in the middle of the room, and beside her, I now noticed JJ's mom, the mayor, and next to them, Veronica and Gus from the TV station.

"Everyone! Welcome!" Mrs. Ryan looked like she'd swallowed sunshine. Her whole face was glowing. "I want to thank you all for coming. About a month ago, a girl named Suki came into the shelter looking for a dog she'd seen in the park."

I blushed at the attention. And felt a little embarrassed, since that was the day I'd found Cinnamon Bun, who turned out not to be Cinnamon Bun at all. I looked down at Sandy, who was lying at JJ's feet, next to Luna.

"She was so concerned about the dog, I knew right away this was a special girl. But I didn't know how special until she began working here. And, then again, I really didn't know how extraordinary Suki was until she donated proceeds to us from her school's Valentine's Day Cupid Notes fund-raiser. We'd be closing our doors forever without her and her friends."

A voice whispered in my ear, "Want to tell her it's Cupid Cards, not Cupid Notes?"

I turned to JJ and chuckled, "Nah."

Mrs. Ryan pointed at the banner behind her head. "All these companies saw the story about the shelter on the news. They've offered donations, and more keep coming." Mrs. Ryan stepped down off the chair and came to me. "We now have enough money to run for several years, and with the mayor's help, for many years after that. Thank you!"

I felt like I might cry if she said anything else. This was better than I'd ever imagined. I sniffled and held back tears. We'd saved the shelter!

"One more thing," Mrs. Ryan said, before ending her speech. She led me to the chair where she'd been standing. "Ben has something to say."

"Really?" Okay, that was weird. What could he possibly have to say?

Ben came over to me, holding the most adorable cream-colored poodle puppy.

"He's yours," Ben said, handing the dog to me.

What? My mom pressed her way through the crowd. Dad was with her.

Dad said, "You've proven you're responsible enough to have a dog."

"Does this mean I'm not grounded, too?" I raised an eyebrow.

"Don't press it." Mom hugged me. "Be grateful."

"Oh, oh, oh," I was so grateful that I was having a hard time making words. "I—" I shook my head. "Wait. Hang on." I took a deep breath and looked over at Mrs. Ryan. "Puppies get adopted easily, right?" She nodded. "So, if this baby will get a good home, can I choose another dog?"

220   CINNAMON BUN BESTIES

I swear there were tears in Mrs. Ryan's eyes as I handed the puppy back to Ben and rushed to the back. With a wink to my favorite carpet/dog, lying unwittingly in his cage, I snagged the photo from the OUR LONGEST RESIDENTS board and came back to the gathering.

"He's a pain in the butt," Ben said, looking at what dog I'd chosen.

"He's my pain now," I chuckled.

"Are you sure?" Mom asked.

"We thought you'd like the puppy," Dad said, glancing at Mrs. Ryan. "Louisa said Bowzer isn't trained well enough to live with a family, and she isn't sure when he'll be ready."

"I'll keep working with him," I told them.

Mom smiled. "And when he's ready to live with us, you can bring him home." She reached out her hand to take Dad's in hers. "Bowzer is your dog, Suki."

I looked at the photo of the monster dog in my hands and that was when the tears that had been threatening to come started to flow.

Before anyone left, Mrs. Ryan led a tour of the shelter. I trailed behind Marley, Ben, Rotem, JJ, and Olivia.

To think . . . just a few weeks ago, my only friend from this group was Marley. I couldn't help but grin when we passed Bowzer's cage. As Mrs. Ryan posted a sign that said SUKI'S DOG on the door, Bowzer gave a weak growl. But when he saw me, he perked up! He actually sat up straight, and I swear he even thumped his tail a few times.

I laughed. This was my dog. And I loved him.

Chapter Twenty-One
BLOBS AND BESTIES

A week after Valentine's Day

I sent each of my besties a blob heart. We'd had a few left over, and I thought it would be funny to hand them out.

I wrote on each one:

Meet me in the park.

Then, I added personal notes to each of them and slipped them into my friends' lockers.

I hadn't signed them, but it was obvious who they were from. So when they all found me standing by the park bench, no one was surprised.

Well, that wasn't totally true.

Everyone was surprised to see who I had with me—Bowzer! He'd been doing so well in his training, I asked Alexandra what she thought of taking him outside. She said she thought it was okay, but that I shouldn't let him get too close to the other dogs. Not yet.

"Is that the new leash I gave you?" JJ asked as he and Sandy came around the bushes by the apartments.

"It is," I called out cheerfully, making sure to keep a good distance away so Bowzer didn't get too close to Sandy. "Do you mind that Bowzer is using it?"

"Of course not, but Sandy might be jealous!"

"Really?" I asked Sandy her thoughts. She gave a little bark. "She says it's okay," I assured JJ. "Sandy likes to share."

On the way, Marley and I had stopped to get Cinnamon Bun Swirl drinks for everyone.

"Thanks. I never had this before," JJ said, taking his cup from the carrier and downing a quick sip. "It's amazing."

"I know." I beamed.

JJ and Sandy walked ahead to where Marley and Rotem were setting up the things I'd asked them to bring.

"Is this an obstacle course?" Ben was helping set a long board onto bricks, like a balance beam.

"The best one you've ever seen," Marley assured him. It was based on Rotem's original plan, slimmed down and without the dog trap.

I tied Bowzer's leash to a big tree, where he could see us but be kept away from the other dogs. Olivia was on her way with Luna.

"This is for you." I spilled a little of my drink onto my fingers and let Bowzer lick it off. I'd never seen the monster so happy.

"You'll get to play with the others someday," I assured him. "A little more training. In the meantime, stay here." I gave the "Stay" command and rushed off to help my friends get ready. He seemed happy enough to just lie down in the cool grass and watch all of the excitement.

"I love this drink," JJ said. "Is that why you called her Cinnamon Bun?" He handed me the cup as he set Sandy up at the starting line.

Wait, how did he know about Cinnamon Bun? I knew that I'd never told him the whole story. I immediately turned to Marley, who gave me a guilty look.

At first, I felt a little embarrassed, and maybe an

echo of being mad at JJ for all those years. But then I took a deep breath and did exactly what my mom told me to do: I opened my heart.

I looked around at my friends, and at the adorable dogs. And JJ—who, yes, I admitted it, was my crush. I was pretty sure the feeling was mutual, too. It just took us three years to figure it out.

I smiled and said, "Yes. Sandy loves that drink, too." Then, since I knew it wasn't healthy, I added, "But she should only have a little. On special occasions."

He smiled and let Sandy lick a few drops off his fingers.

When Olivia arrived, the course was nearly set up. I had treats in my pocket from the shelter.

JJ lined up Sandy at the start. I called out, "Ready? Set? Go!" And JJ released Sandy's leash. He ran alongside her as she went through the obstacle course—over the board, under another board, through the hoops, around some cones, and across the finish line. Then JJ put her leash back on, saying, "That was fun!"

While Sandy rested up for her next run, Ben straightened everything out on the course, and Olivia started getting Luna ready for her turn.

Suddenly, JJ reached out and took my hand in his.

We stood like that for a long moment, not saying anything. My heart was pounding, in a good way. The charms on my bracelet jingled when he swung my hand gently back and forth.

"Are you two going to stand there all day?" Marley shouted to us. She was with Rotem, sitting on the bench. He was timing the dogs and making adjustments to the "schematics" for a better obstacle course.

"Come on!" Olivia called. She had Luna set at the starting line. "Ready? Set?"

I looked at JJ, and at the same exact moment, we both yelled "GO!"

Don't miss any Swirl novels! Read on for a sneak peek at *Salted Caramel Dreams*

For the next hour, everything is perfect. With the music flowing, I relax, letting myself sing along to the Top 40 station as my stitches become tighter, the beads even straighter than I was able to get last night. *I can't wait to use this at school*, I think, happy to have an excuse to retire my practical—yet very boring—purple backpack I've had since I was ten. My bag is a perfect copy of one I saw online for hundreds of dollars.

"This is looking phenomenal," Ms. Chloe says, surprising me from behind. "You're a real natural at this, Jasmine. Truly, you have such an eye."

I look down and smile. "Thanks, Ms. Chloe."

"No, thank *you*. I can't wait to buy one of your Jasmine originals," she says with a wink.

By the time class ends, I'm just a few touches away from finishing, and wish I could stay another hour. But dinner at home is always at six, so lingering isn't an option. I grab my coat, and Kiara and I head toward the staircase.

"Well that was fun," Kiara says as we reach the street. "I just can't believe today might've been my last class. I'll know if I made the basketball team by the end of the week!"

"Wow. That's right," I say, and for a second I start to worry all over again.

But Kiara snaps me out of it. "By the way," she says, "I totally forgot to ask you about your latest pattern. Any update?"

I smile as I picture the pinned together fabric scraps I've assembled on the dress form in my closet—which is really just a secondhand mannequin Mom found for me in a thrift store.

"Not much new," I say as we cross Main Street and begin the short walk to our neighborhood. "Still working on it."

"I'm sure you'll get it soon," she says.

"We'll see," I say. "It can't end up worse than the micro-dresses."

We erupt into laughter as we think of the matching sundresses I tried to make last summer. They were supposed to have short sleeves and fall to our knees, and I got this pretty Hawaiian print fabric to make them with. But after pinning the fabric and taking measurements and creating a pattern, I forgot to cut extra fabric for seams. So the sleeves had come out too narrow for us to fit our arms in. And the skirt length was way too short—the dresses barely hit our thighs! Talk about a disaster. The only thing I'd been able to save was a little of the fabric, which I'd used on one of my bags as trim.

"On second thought, maybe you should just stick with the bags," says Kiara.

"Seriously. The patterns sure are easier," I say.

And then before I can think about it anymore,

we're at the top of the hill. The spot where we always part ways.

Kiara extends her hand, breaking me away from my thoughts.

"Tick tock, tick tock . . ." she begins.

"Who's the coolest on the block?" I say, slapping her hand with mine. Then we entwine our fingers and laugh before completing the secret handshake we've been perfecting since the fourth grade.

"Well, I'll see you tomorrow, girl," Kiara says with a smile.

"I'll be here, ready to go at seven," I say.

"Can't wait! And don't forget. Friday—sleepover at my place. No matter what," Kiara says, turning back toward her street.

After a quick wave, I do the same. Picking up my pace, I zip my coat a little higher, trying to keep out the cold. The evening air is sharper than it was just last week, a sign of the changing season. I think of Kiara's last words: *Friday. Sleepover. No matter what.* Their warmth hugs me tight as my cheery yellow house comes into focus. I turn into the driveway and breathe in deep, preparing for the chaos that comes with having two parents, twin brothers, and a live-in grandma. Yet as I reach for the doorknob, I find my mind's still filled with doubt. Because as great as this basketball thing may turn out to be for Kiara, I can't quite shake the sinking feeling that things are really about to change.

SWIRL

Swirl books are the perfect flavor: A sweet blend of
friends, crushes, and fun. Curl up and take a sip!

Sky Pony Press
New York

About the Author

Stacia Deutsch has written more than two hundred children's books. She started her career with the award-winning chapter book series Blast to the Past, and recent publications include The Mysterious Makers of Shaker Street series and the *New York Times* bestselling Girls Who Code series. She lives in Irvine, California. Find her online at www.staciadeutsch.com.